YOUR IMAGINATION CAN BE YOUR DREAM, IF YOU FOLLOW IT
WITHOUT FEAR-JJ

1

"Wow! So that's how you do me, June? We make theses plans, and you still turn me down."

"Well, Terrell. I really didn't think you would come pick me up. We been flirting for months, and it hasn't gone any further than that."

Setting up from laying on Terrells chest. June starts to adjust her position so she can look Terrell in his eye's for sympathy.

"Besides, now is not the time for me to lose my virginity, Terrell."

"Next time don't ask me to come get you if you're not down. You were talking all that game yesterday at school, and now you ain't living up to the hype. So, trust me when I tell you I'm pissed off witcha."

Getting up from his side of the bed. Terrell starts putting his socks, and shoes back on. Completely frustrated by Junes playful tactics, he was ready to go. But, to be sure she hadn't changed her mind; he made one more attempt before leaving his cousin's house to get what he originally came for.

"Can I at least get some head? I mean, man! I didn't drive all this way for nothing. That's not sex is it?" Terrell laughed, in hopes that what he was asking for wasn't too far fetch.

June didn't crack as smile. "I do believe that's still sex Terrell. Hold up! We only fifteen minutes away from my job, so what's the big deal? Why are you in such a rush?"

"Because, I still have other things to do, and since ain't shit going down here, we might as well go. Unless you want to use that brain and think long, hard, and deep about what you really want to do. But, if it's not going down, then I really don't have time to waste."

June started to feel some type of way about Terrell's reaction. She knew the whole time she wasn't ready to have sex, but thought by being enticing it would be the only way to get Terrells full attention. She started to change her mind, and follow through with the jester of oral sex. But, once she heard the tone in his voice she knew she made the right decision.

Still sitting on her side of the bed, she watched Terrell put his shirt on, and grab his keys. *Let me get out this bed.* June thought, as she slowly made her way to the center of the room. She took a minute to buckle her pants that were never fully removed, and to roll down her shirt that Terrell tried to take off. They both stood face to face, as Terrell kisses June on the forehead to show he was no longer angry. June couldn't do anything but smile, and think about her true feelings for Terrell, as they went down the stairs, and out the front door.

Terrell made conversation to break the silence, as they walked to his car.

"June, I still can't believe you're a virgin at eighteen. I mean, really! We're grown."

"We're eighteen Terrell, and still live with our parents. So, how is that considered grown? To me, that's still young. Don't get me wrong, we are young adults, but grown no. And, why can't you believe I'm a virgin? Is something wrong with that? I take honor in being a virgin at my age. It's the one thing I have full control over, and can save for the man of my dreams."

"Then why do you flirt so much if you know it's not going nowhere?"

"I don't know, Terrell. I like to flirt a lot, big deal. But, that doesn't mean I have to give it up."

June knew one day her flirty ways would catch up with her. She just never thought it would get this instance, and with the boy she had a crush on since she moved to Waco Texas from Pontiac, Michigan.

"No, you don't have to give it up, but I will say you're a tease."

Terrell paused for a minute, while still slowly walking across the driveway. He didn't want to blow his future chancing of getting June, so he knew a compliment was in order. He opens her side of the car door, and June eased in. She then reached over to the driver side handle, and gave it a slight push.

"You're still sexy as hell, June." Terrell said as he eased his seatbelt on, with an undoubting grin. He started the car and left it idle, so the a/c could blow.

"I mean, look at you. Those big brown eyes, naturally curly hair, long sexy legs, and don't let me get started on that hour glass figure. Damn! Girl, you got a body! Hell, who wouldn't try to hit that."

"Go on." June replies, flattered by Terrells compliments.

"I still want to hit that, but you're too damn confusing at times. And, please don't take that the wrong why. But, for instance. We flirt all day at school. Then we set up this plan to meet up for one on one time, because I can never come to your house. And, from what you said your mother won't let you come to mine, so today was the perfect opportunity. But, you didn't want to take it. Then, you suppose to be at work and you here with me. That's why today I thought is was really about to go down. But, you playing. What's up? You don't want me?"

"To be truthful Terrell, I thought you were my boyfriend, and you would be the dream guy to lose my virginity to. So, I didn't see nothing wrong with taking things slow, and missing a day of work for you. I mean… We did make out, which was major in my book. I just didn't have enough guts to go all the way. What's so wrong with that?"

7

"Stop making the assumption that we're a couple. Just because we talk from time to time. That doesn't mean we're together."

"Eight and a half months of just talking Terrell, but I guess I'm the only one who's counting. You see, this is why I'm still a virgin, because guys like you feel that females like me should just give it up on their demand. Then y'all won't even honor the fact of putting a label on the relationship."

"Yeah, and females like you, feel since we talk from time to time that we're in a relationship, but then want to play games when it comes down to doing what people in a relationship do."

"Every day is just talking from time to time to you, Terrell?"

"June, I've never seen you outside of school. We've never been on a date, you're always buried in some book. And, the times I did see you, you were with a group of friends. Which, me and my boys just tag along. So, how is that a relationship?

June just sat with a puzzled look on her face. She pulled out her phone to check the time, because she didn't want to be late going back to work, and to make sure she didn't have any missed calls from her mother.

"Whatever."

Was the only thing she could think to reply back, because she knew there was some truth to his statement. But, still felt that her time with Terrell deserved a label.

"Take me back to work. I need to be back before my shift is over."

"Sure, that's no problem. We can just meet up tomorrow. If you want to."

"Really?"

"What?"

"You just said, don't make an assumption about this relationship."

"So."

June couldn't help but to let her eyes roll to the back
of her head. Knowing exactly why he wanted to meet
tomorrow, but still wanted to hear his reason.

"So, why do you want to meet up tomorrow?

"You know why. Same time, same place. I mean, if
that's cool with you?

June shrugs her shoulders. "Yeah, we can meet up,
but ain't nothing coming off, or going down."

The car grew silent as Terrell pulled off, and focused
on the road. With each passing light, June mentally went over
her thoughts about Terrell, and if he was really who she
thought he was.

"What do you plan on telling your boss why you
missed your shift today, if he's there when you come back? It
really doesn't sound like a solid plan to me."

"You don't have to worry about that, Terrell. You just
drive this Toyota Corolla, and make sure I'm there on time."

"Yes, ma'am, and you sassy too, and you know I like that, don't you."

They both laughed, as Terrell gets in the turning line in front of Toni's Pizza Plaza. Waiting at the red light. June quickly ducks her head lower in the passenger seat.

"What's wrong witcha?"

"Oh Lord!" Terrell, that's my mother's car! Why was she here? What are we going to do?"

"We? You mean, you. What you gon do? That's your mother, not mine. I can hit a couple of blocks fo ya, if you don't want me to pull in. But, after that I'm gon home."

"Home?" June eye's lowered, and her cheeks grew red. "You said that like that wasn't your house, or your bed, we were laying in?"

"It wasn't, it was my cousin's house. But, that's something you shouldn't be worried about at this point in time. The question is still remains. What you gon tell yo momma?"

"I really don't know, but I'll think of something. Just drop me off."

Fear over takes June's body, because she knew she wasn't a good liar, but at this point she couldn't tell her mother the truth. Terrell then makes the right turn, and drives down to the corner of the ABC store.

"I'ma drop you off over here, so you won't be directly in front of the pizza bar. That way my car is completely out of sight, and you can just walk up the street and make the corner. But, call me if you're not in too much trouble, or shoot me a text so I know you made it home. Damn, girl, I hope you be aight."

"I will. Be safe Terrell."

"I gotcha."

Terrell rode pass, concerned about how her night would end, as June walked around the corner of the ABC store in complete terror. She knew her mother wasn't at the pizza bar, but she had no alibi as to why she wasn't at work when her mother showed up.

What will I tell my mother? I got five minutes until I make it home. Man, why did she even come to the store.

June was trying to wrap her mind around the situation while taking a quick glance in the building. That way she could use one of her coworkers to make her story sound more believable.

Amber's house is right up the street, and she's not working today from my quick view. So, I'll use her. Which, I know she'll cover for me if my mother calls. Seeing that she's the only other person mom likes at my job, besides Bill.

Walking down the street felt like the green mile to June, as She starts to make her way up the driveway. She constantly repeated the story in her head to be sure she didn't forget anything. Her shirt became obsessively wet under her armpits. The hairs on her face even stood up at the idea of confronting her mother, and she no longer could feel the pit of her stomach. To say she was overwhelmed with adrenaline would be an understatement. Her hands were shaking so bad, that she could barely put in the passcode to open the gate.

I'm more scared now, than when I was with Terrell. I really need to get it together, so she believes this one. The last time I got in trouble mom said, "she took it easy on me." so I know this will be deadly. The front door swung open before June could even push it completely through, causing her to stumble in.

"Hey Ma, how was your day?"

"It was good June, and yours?"

"Um, it was okay."

"So, we really gon play this game June?" Mrs. Avery replied, "We gon sit here, like I didn't just leave your job, and you weren't there."

Dawn Avery's tone grew louder as more words came out of her mouth. She was the kind of mother that showed her daughter just enough leeway for her to feel like a young adult, but at the same time, she kept her on a tight leash. She also made it her duty to keep a close track on June's social life, her whereabouts, and the people she hung out with. While still maintaining multiple hours at the Girls Behavioral Camp, where she worked. Which made her worries worse, because she lived by the stories told at the boot camp. Although, she adored the girls that come through there. She was doing her best to be sure that her daughter didn't end up that way.

"Where the hell were you June? And I dare you to fix your lips to lie to me, I will slap them clean off your face."

"I took a late lunch, and went to Amber's house for a minute."

"So, that's what you did?"

Dawn already knew she was lying, because she had already taken the liberty of calling Ambers mother to check and see if June was there, but Amber wasn't home herself.

"Let me call Amber's mother to make sure you're not lying."

Dawn gave June another chance to tell the truth before she suffered the consequences of her anger.

June finally sighs with relief, as her mother walks through the living room, and into the hallway. Trailing slowly behind her. June sat in the hallway chair while her mother reached for the phone.

I guess I'm in the clear. Mothers facial express hasn't changed, but I'm sure once Amber tells her the same story, things will turn around. I've never seen mother this anger before. She walked pass me several times without saying anything, and her eyes were red as if she was crying, then she interrupted me before I could even explain to her that I was with Amber.

June looked up to see if her mother was still on the phone, and Mrs. Avery didn't hold back from slapping her clean across the face.

"What did I do? Why did you hit me?"

"For lying, and don't question me again, or I'll make it worse than a slap."

"Mom, I promise! I went to Amber's house for lunch." June replies with a ringing ear, and her face pounding.

"June! Please just stop! I cannot believe you're continuing to lie right in my face. I really thought I raised you better than that. Which, I can see I haven't. Now! I'm going to test you again, and all I really need to know is one thing. Did he wear a condom, or not?"

"Condom!"

June eyes couldn't catch a break from being in fear, and she could know longer hold back her tears.

I'll be dead soon, real soon, so let me just tell the truth, or maybe I should just stick to my story? I'm busted anyway, so at this point it really don't matter. I'll just stick to my story. I'm already in too deep to change things. June mind was still on overload, but she still choose to go down fighting.

"Mother, what are you talking about?"

"June, what you fail to realize is that your boss, Bill. You remember him? While he was taking the trash out. He saw you ride off with some boy in a blue Corolla. Where y'all were going, he didn't know, but he did know that I did not allow that kind of behavior to take place, and so do you. And by the way, it's not cool to drag your friend in your BS. Amber wasn't even home, while you were out doing your dirt. So, yes! My dear, I already called Ambers mother before you got here. So, from jump street. I knew you were lying. Now, where did y'all go? And did he wear a condom?"

I might as well tell her the truth now, because death is upon me, and I can't believe my mother would think I'm just out there having sex with just anybody.

"Yes, ma'am!! I mean no ma'am, no sex was had, so no condom was needed, and we went to what I think was his house."

"June! I really can't believe you. Do you know how unsafe that was? Do you hear yourself? "What I think was his house." Have you lost your damn mind? You could've been kidnapped, raped, murdered any of those things, trying to do what? Chase after some nappy headed boy. I'm beyond furious, I'm livid just thinking about it. Answer me, child! Don't you hear me talking to you?"

Dawn gave June no time for a response. "June! Why should I believe you? You just trollop yo ass in here like nothing happened, and lied straight to my face. How do I know you didn't have sex? How?" Angry took over, and rage sat in. Mrs. Avery had to take a step back from being in Junes face.

"But, Mom."

"But, mom nothing. June, listen."

Dawn did her best to lower her voice, and in full frustration took a deep breath. She headed over to the kitchen to grab a bottle of water, and an ice pack. Slowly sipping her water, she tried to calm herself down. Still pacing back and forth, she felt it was best for her to go upstairs, and take her anxiety pills, and June had no choice but to follow. Once in her room. Dawn sat on the bedroom bench, and June stood in her mother's doorway with her head down, and a cold ice pack that covered the right side of her face.

"Little girl!" Dawn said with her hands in the praying formation. "I need you to understand. Just because I work all these hours, and be asleep. Doesn't mean, I don't know what's going on in your life. I am still your mother, and will always be. I will always know what's going on with you, even before you do. So, before I let this belt do the talking, and inform your father about what's going on, is there anything else I need to know?" Dawn finally gave June the floor, so she could respond to her questions, but June was just standing in a daze.

I really thought my mom would be proud of me, because I didn't have sex. I feel like whether I did, or didn't. She still would've been mad at me, and I wonder why Terrell hasn't called, or texted me? Does he really care, or is all this truly about sex for him?

"June, I'm talking to you." Dawn jumps up after getting no response from June.

"No, ma'am." June replies fast, but with a very low tone. "I mean! What I'm saying mom. Yes, I know you don't believe me at this moment, but I promise you mother nothing happened. We kissed, and he brought me back to work, and that's all. Mom, believe me, nothing else happened.

"June! I don't believe you? And don't say nothing happened, because kissing, and hugging is something. Kissing and hugging leads to sex June. Hell, how you think you got here."

"I guess you're right, mom. I wouldn't believe me either, but it's the truth."

June, wiping tears away from her eyes still couldn't understand what danger she put her life in. She then went and sat in the same spot her mother was sitting in.

"Let me tell you something little girl." Dawn sat back down, and grabbed Junes hand, to assure June that this was a serious matter. "Sex is something you just can't play with. Yes, I understand that it may seem fun, and what y'all young folks take lightly, but it brings a lot of problems as well. I'm sure you know about STD's, your name being tossed around in your school, the streets, and other places. I'm sure you know of some young female hoes in your school. Dare I mention pregnancy young lady, and if you bring a child in this house." Dawn paused for a minute, with the thought of her teenage daughter being a teenage mother. "I'm sorry my dear, but you will have to go. Do I make myself clear?"

June sat quiet as Dawn looked her square in the eyes, and she could tell her mother was very hurt, let alone disappointed.

"Yes, ma'am. I get what you're saying mom, I completely understand."

"Well, I'm glad you understand, because first thing in the morning we're going to the health clinic to get you checked out." Dawn walked away after patting June on the shoulder. "Damn! June, now I have to explain this to your father. And, you know how he deals with these things." Dawn then re-entered into the room, after leaving her closet space, and ordered June to lay across the bed. "You already know the deal. Go ahead and lie across this bed, because you're not getting away with this one without a good ass whopping."

2

The steam from the shower filled the bathroom as June stepped out, and wrapped the towel around her chest. She could no longer withstand the hot heat on the welts that crossed the back of her legs, and her buttocks. Leaning in to clean the mirror, she didn't hesitate to wipe the familiar tears that filled her face.

I can't believe I'm eighteen, and still got a whooping. I'm too old for this. Then, Terrell didn't even bother to call and check on me. But, I guess I can understand since he didn't know how much trouble I would be in. I hope I haven't played too many games with him, because I truly care about him.

"June," Mrs. Avery screams from the bottom of the stairwell.

"Yes, ma'am."

"Hurry up, and get dressed for school. I don't want to be late for your appointment."

"I'm going to school to?"

"Oh, yes ma'am! I have to go to work, and you're not missing school, because you out here trying to be fast. So, get your stuff together, so we can go."

June stepped out the bathroom door, so she could hear her mother more clearly without all the screaming.

"Mom, why do I have to do both?"

"June, I said to get your stuff together, and don't let me have to tell you again."

What's up with mom this morning? June said to herself, as she dried off, and started to get dressed. She's so moody, I can't deal with her this morning. I don't want to go to this nasty clinic myself, and besides, it was her idea anyway. So, why is she mad at me. If she would've just believed me when I told her, we didn't do anything. I would be at school right now.

Snatching her school bag, she slowly walked down stairs, and out to the car where her mother was waiting.

"Mom, I have one last question."

"What?"

"Are you mad at me?"

"June, I'm not mad at you. I'm just very disappointed with you. I've taught you better than this. And for you to just lie to someone, let alone it be your mother, is very disrespectful. You have crossed all barriers this time, and I won't stand for it. Let's start with the fact that you missed work. You then lied about it, not only to me, but your boss. I'm not even gon bring up the boy, because it will make me mad all over again"

Dawn shakes her head. "Don't get me wrong, I understand that you're a teenager, and want to be with your peers, but it's still a more dignified way to handle things. Like coming to your parents, and letting us know that you're into boys sexually. That way we, meaning you and I can handle things properly. I thought we had a better relationship than this. I really felt like we could tell each other anything. But, I guess I was wrong. Now, not going to your father on the other hand, I could understand. I stayed up all night explaining to him that you didn't have sex, and was still a virgin. Right, you are still a virgin? Which it don't matter, because we are here now. And, these test results will explain everything."

"Well, I just want to say, sorry mom. I am very sorry, and it won't happen again."

"Well it better not young lady. Not if you under my roof, and it's not what you did, it's how you did it."

"Will I be able to keep my job?"

"I don't know. We will discuss these things with your father at tonight's dinner, but until then let's just see how this check up goes."

June and Dawn get out the car at Waco Medical Clinic/Hospital. Just like any other medical hospital it was packed with patients. Dawn rushes to the sign in counter, leaving behind a stagnant June.

Man it's cold in here, and it smells. June thought to herself as she stood by her mother at the sign in desk. She couldn't help but notice how clean it was, but at the same time it smelled so dirty.

"Lord, please don't let me be in here long." June spoke quietly, as she sat down.

"Johnson," the nurse yells out.

"June get your stuff together your next."

"Avery" the nurse screams again.

June couldn't speak from pure dismay, as she gathered her things.

It just got real. Not even two minutes passed, and my name has been called. What am I going to do? I'm scared. I don't think I can do this, I am truly about to piss my pants. Wait! Why am I scared? I keep asking myself that. I didn't do anything, but kiss him, and the last I heard kissing didn't produce babies.

June got up slowly with her knees buckling. The nurse places her in a room with diagrams of the female body. Two walls were painted pink, and the two others cream. Giving the room a more wholesome feel, which is was suppose to give the clients comfort. There were so many tools lying around, and jars full of cotton balls, gloves, and large tubs of cream. The room was just as cold as the lobby, but smelled much better.

"I hate pink. Mom, I'm ready to go."

Mrs. Avery completely ignores Junes rant, as she gets up, and looks in a couple more cabinets while waiting for the doctor.

"Girl, be quiet and wait for the doctor to come in."

Mrs. Avery said, as she sat next to June. Minutes later there was a small tap on the door, before it swung open. And, as Mrs. Avery requested a female doctor walked in.

"Hi, June! I am Dr. Aldis Brown, I will be completing your exams today. How are you?" Dr. Aldis Brown extended her hand to June, and also to Mrs. Avery.

"I'm good, I am a little cold, and scared. But, I'll be fine."

Her voice became shaky, and her mother could only give a look of why, especially since nothing happened, according to June. Which only left her blaming this on how cold the room was, as she completely ignored the expression on her mother's face.

"Well, that's normal to be a little nervous." said Dr. Aldis, as she places her charts on the counter, and pulls her chair closer. Dr. Aldis begins to perform the normal testing after putting her gloves on, which consist of searching her ears, eyes, and throat.

"I have a couple of questions to ask you first, then we can move on with the other exams, okay!"

June eyes were wide with concern, and more fear. Dr. Aldis Brown removes her gloves, and jots down a couple notes.

"Yes, ma'am." She replies, after making contact with her mother. The expression on her face spoke volumes to say. Dang, that wasn't the test. But, Dawn just gave June a shoulder nod, as she put her magazine to the side, so she could pay close attention to the real exam that was about to take place.

"Since you're eighteen, it's your choice if you want your mother in the room. This part is totally up to you."

"Don't worry, I'm not going anywhere." Replies Mrs. Avery.

"Mom, please." June states, as she holds her head down, looking at the flooring from the hospital bed.

"June, I can't believe you want me to leave."

"Well, Mrs. Avery I'm going to have to ask you to step out." Spoke Dr. Brown as she held the door open for Dawn.

"Well, damn!" Says Mrs. Avery in disbelief, as she grabs her purse, and walks towards the lobby.

"June, I'm going to ask you some questions now that your mothers gone." Dr. Aldis sits in her chair with her chart, and pen, ready to write down all information given.

"Your full name is June Denise Avery, correct."

"Yes, ma'am."

"You were born in Waco, Texas, your 5'5, brown eyes, and you're here to take a virginity test? Is that correct?"

"No, ma'am. Pontiac, Michigan is where I'm originally from, but the rest is true "

"So, have you ever been sexually active?"

"No, ma'am, I've kissed a couple of times, but that's it. I can say, I have been in some uncomfortable situations, but never touched by a boy."

"Would you care to discuss what you mean by uncomfortable situations?"

"No, ma'am. I'm good on that one, maybe some other time."

"I can't make you discuss those situations, but if anything non-consensual has happened to you please report it to our confidential hotline. It's totally free, and they will lead you in the best direction. Responses like that concern me as a doctor, and I always have your best interest at heart when I ask for this information. Are we clear on that?"

"Yes, ma'am!"

"And, if at anytime you like to talk to me, please feel free to call me. Secondly. Do you have a boyfriend?"

"Yes, ma'am, his name is Terrell, and he goes to my school."

"Is he sexually active?"

"No, ma'am! Not that I know of, but that's why I'm here. My mom is under the impression that we had sex."

"Did you two have sex, which also includes oral? I know that may seem a little uncomfortable, but I have to ask. Most young adults don't understand that oral sex is still sex."

"No! I completely understand, but no ma'am. I haven't had any kind of sex at all, and I plan to keep it that way. Well, at least until I'm ready."

"How does Terrell feel about that?"

"I really don't know, we never talked about it, for real."

"Well! Always remember these are the top three things you should know about your mate. One, know if he's sexually active. Two, ask him if he's ever had any STD'S, and lastly, when was the last time he visited his doctor, or been tested. Which all these things are to protect you June.

Which, Terrell shouldn't have a problem answering these questions, and if he does, he's not the right one."

"Yes, ma'am." June replied, still thinking. How am I going to ask Terrell these questions? For one, I'm too scared, and two, he feels we are not a couple. But, whatever! I'll ask him anyway.

"Now I need you to remove all clothing. Once that is complete, you will then lay back, and prop your feet up, and slide down to the edge of the bed."

June followed Dr. Aldis orders, as she closed the curtains, and completed her notes.

"Last night really wasn't worth this," June stated as she laid her head on the cold plastic bed.

"Well, always keep those things in mind when making life changing decisions. There is, and will always be an outcome." Dr. Aldis says, as she re-enters the curtains with new gloves, and a couple unfamiliar tools in her hand.

The first part began with a breast exam. Dr. Brown examined every part of her breast from under her armpit to the tip of her nipples all in a circular motion. She then lowered her exam to the pelvic area where things became more painful. June legs were already open, from the stirrups, and Dr. Brown didn't waste any time rolling in between her legs. The exam light was warm as is shined directly into her pelvic area.

"You're going to feel my hands going down your thigh as I use the speculum to open up your vagina."

June's only response was. "Ouch," as the exam continued to take place.

"Now you'll feel a cold lubricant from the cotton swab, and the exam will be almost over."

"Yes, ma'am." June replied with one arm over her eyes and the other hand gripping the bed.

Doctor Aldis stood up, as she placed more lubricant on her index, and middle finger to check the cervix, and other vaginal internal areas. She then orders June to take a deep breath, as she removed the speculum.

"Now that wasn't so bad was it?" Dr. Brown asked as she helped June up from the bed.

"Yes, ma'am! It was."

"I'm sorry honey." Dr. Aldis smiled, as she walks to the trash to throw her gloves away, and send her swab off for testing.

I'm so glad that's over. This has been the most uncomfortable situation, I have been in. I would rather stay a virgin then go through this again.

June's thoughts were flying all over her head as she sat up from the cold plastic exam bed, with the blue thin lace plastic bed covers, that wrapped around her body.

"Mrs. Brown, is there any towels I can use to clean myself up. I have to go to school when I leave here."

"No towels dear, but there are some wet wipe's, and thick paper towels that will remove some of that lubricant.

You can use the ones on the counter. I'm stepping out, and I'll be back with your results shortly."

Dr. Aldis walked out, and June cleaned herself up. Using the paper towels, and the warm water from the sink. She sat back on the cold bed where her examination took place fully dressed, and waiting for Dr. Brown to return.

"I feel humiliated." June said as the door swung open fifteen minutes later.

"Why?" Replied Dr. Aldis. "You really shouldn't. Everything looks good, and from my results you are still a virgin. I do have some pamphlets for you to read over, and if you want to get on any contraceptives please feel free to ask. But, like I've said before. No sex is the best contraceptive, but you're old enough to make that decision."

"My mother is going to kill me, but I would like to get on birth control for menstrual purposes."

"That's understandable."

After searching thought some of the cabinets. Dr. Aldis, hands June some brochures, and a couple of samples.

"Here's the daily plan for the pills, and the birth control. Take these samples today to get you started, and be sure to take them at the same time each day for them to be more effective. Now! I have one last question for you, which is a little personal. So, at this moment I'm taking off my Dr. Cape, and I'm just Mrs. Aldis Brown, or Mrs. Brown to you."

June just remains silent, but nods her head in agreement. She knew this most of been really important, because she actually removed her white doctor's robe.

"This young man Terrell, who goes to Waco High. Is he about 5'8, brown skin, built kind of stocky, yet toned with dreads, and brown hazel eyes?"

"Um, yes, ma'am! How did you know?" June replied. Listening closely to every word that was about to come out of Mrs. Browns mouth.

Okay, this is weird, and my eyes have frozen with confusion, and yet embarrassment. What just happened here? Did I tell her too much information? Does she know him? Oh man! Is he one of her clients? This exam has taken at left real quick. June expressed her thoughts with her eyes.

"June!" Mrs. Aldis snaps her fingers, bringing June back into reality. "There is no need to be embarrassed, or confused. I am his mother, and I will not discuss any of your information with him. I will protect your privacy by all means, but when you said you attended Waco High, and with your age group. I could only assume you were talking about my son. I must say, it was nice to meet one of his lady friends who still has morals. Now if there are no more questions, you are free to go." Aldis shakes June hand, and assist her with the door, as she showed June the way out.

"I didn't get him in any trouble. Did I?"

"No, ma'am" Mrs. Aldis replies. "Now don't forget to stop by the receptionist to set up your next appointment, and call me anytime if you have any questions, or concerns."

"Yes, ma'am."

That's his mother. O.M.G!! I just meet his mother. I really thought it would be under different circumstances, but oh well. I hope she doesn't tell him I was here, or any of my information. But, Mrs. Brown is so cute. She looks so young, 45 at the oldest maybe 50, with her long hair, petite waist, and she can't be over 5'7. Dang! Now that I think about it, they almost look like twins. They both have that good honey brown skin tone, and those hazel brown eye's. How could I not tell? I guess, cause I never even thought about his parents. The whole eight months of use getting to know each other, we never talked about our home situation. We always meet at the park, or at a mutual friend's house. So, it was kind of nice to meet someone tied to Terrells home life.

41

June walked into the lobby with a brown paper bag, and reading the information for her next appointment.

"Are you okay?" Dawn reacted with an attitude, as June looked up at her mother where she was waiting impatiently.

"Yes, mother. I'm fine! As a matter of fact, I'm great."

"That sounds good. "Great," was not the response I was looking for, but I'm glad everything went as we planned. It did go as we planned? Right! Is there anything you would like to talk about?"

"Mom! We haven't even got to the car yet, and we're already playing 21 questions."

"I won't ask you any more questions. Since you didn't want me in the back room with you. I guess you grown now." Dawn replied, as sarcastically as possible.

"Mom, I am grown. When are you going to let go?"

"Never! And, you know I was supposed to stay in there with you. Now let's get you off to school, you've already missed two blocks it's 11:15. June, please stay a virgin until you're married. That will make your mother very proud."

"Yes, ma'am" June replies, as her mother drives off. A couple of miles later, and more questions from her mother, they pull up to the school. From the outside they could hear the bell ring, just in time for the second block.

"Have a great rest of the day my love, and your dad will be here to pick you up. Please come out the same way you went in." June just laughed at the petty joke her mother told.

"Okay mother." June closes the door, and walks to the driver side.

"Love you mom!"

"Love you too dear!"

Dawn pulls off, and heads off to work, as June walks into school shameful. Although, she had high hopes that know one knew what happened last night, and that the

remainder of her time will fly by.

3

"Hey June! What's up girl? Where you been?"

"Hey Stephanie, I been home just running late, that's all."

"Damn! Two whole blocks later. Hell, nah! Something happened. Why you sound sad?"

"OH NO! I'm good," June replies, trying to put some spunk in her voice.

This girl can't take nothing I say face value. I know she my best friend, but she's always in my business. I mean, It's like she can detect when something's wrong.

June just sat back in her thoughts ready for this day to be over, but couldn't get past what just happened last night, and early this morning.

"Well, you shouldn't be good!"

"Why shouldn't I be good, Stephanie?"

"You do know what Terrell is going around the school telling people, don't you?"

See, this is where the drama begins. I know it wouldn't take long for Terrell to go around telling people what happen. This is why I stay to myself. The one boy I finally like, and feel is up to my potential has to act ignorant, but I need to play it cool before I lose it.

"No, girl what he say?"

"Girl! He said, that y'all rode around last night while you gave him head."

"Really! Well, that's a lie, but go on!" June just started shaking her head.

"I knew it wasn't true, but I had to ask you for myself. I mean, y'all have been getting pretty close. He walks you to class and shit, y'all holding hands and shit, being all booed up and shit, y'all more than on a friend tip, if you ask me."

Stephanie made sure June was well aware that she had been paying attention to her, and Terrell's relationship. They both started laughing, but deep down June knew nothing was funny about the situation.

"Girl, Terrell be playing, and I'm just going along with his games. Nothing more, nothing less. It's just that simple." June smiled to contain her tears. She wasn't ready just yet to share how she truly felt about Terrell with Stephaine.

"Yeah! Yeah, so you say. I can tell you like him, ain't nothing wrong with that, he alright."

"How can you tell Steph?"

"Bitch! We have been friends for almost a year now, I do believe I know a little bit about you, and your feelings. Terrell tho! He cute, or whatever, but damn! You know he a playboy, and you can do a whole lot better.

"Lol, Steph, you crazy! Where is his dumb ass anyway?" June asked, trying to act like she didn't care.

"His mother came, and picked him. I thought he was in the office when you checked in, but y'all most have missed each other in the halls."

"So he's gone?"

"But you don't like him." Stephanie replies with laughter, as she gave June a head twist.

"Yeah! Your right, I do like him just a little, and I don't know why. And yes, I'm checking for him." They both got up from her cafeteria seat, as the bell rings again.

"We need to be headed to class Steph."

"Girl, yes we do! Now let's take our butt's to class before the third bell catches us, because you know I can't afford to get in no more trouble if I want to graduate."

June didn't even respond trying to reflect on the information that was given to her by Stephanie. They both walked into the room, and took their seats. June was still lost in her thoughts. Looking out the classroom window, trying to piece everything together.

Terrell is going around the school telling people I gave him head, which is not cool. I didn't think he would treat me that way, but it is what it is. I can't focus on that stuff right now if I want to remain an honor student. I wonder why his mother came to pick him up early? And, it was right after our encounter. Why am I so pissed off right now. I hope his mother doesn't tell him about today. This sucks right now. I'm stuck in this class, and can't concentrate, because I'm worried about this loser. Man, I hope this whole school catches on fire, so I can go home.

June just continues to look out the class window with tears in her eyes.

Dang, I have to deal with dad, and his craziness. This day can't get any worse.

June rested her head on her desk hoping by the time she wakes up from her nap school will be over.

4

"Terrell, what in the hell were you thinking?"

"Mom, what are you talking about?"

"Don't act as if you don't know. Wednesday you told me you, and a couple of your friends were going to play basketball after school, since y'all didn't have practice. Come to find out you was with some girl? Trying to have sex. Really! Terrell?"

"Please, mom!" Terrell smiled, being playful with his mother.

"Terrell, I'm not laughing. I'm very serious, what happened? I need to know the truth."

"Yes, mom. It's true! So what!"

"So, what! Terrell, you not about to be laid up with these girls, and think it's ok. We already got Ally, I don't want any more grandchildren Terrell. None! She's almost three now, and of course I love her, but I can't handle another child. Do you understand?"

"Yes," Terrell replies, unconcern. "Mother, I get it. But, it was your choice to keep Ally, and raise her as yours, instead of my own daughter. Not mine! I wish I would have found my own place to live like Stephanie did, so things wouldn't be this way."

"You think it comes just that easy, don't you Terrell?"

"No, but I know we would've been ok. Where is miss pretty Ally anyway?"

"She's upstairs taking a nap. Her nanny said she was full throttle today, but you still haven't answered my question."

"No, mom! I didn't have sex. She's still the same little virgin I picked up." Terrell says with hostility.

"First, correct your tone young man, and she better be." Mrs. Brown replies, as she kisses her son on the forehead, and walks away to make prep dinner.

"Mom, where's dad?"

"He's at work, of course. To my surprise, I didn't have as many clients today. So, I packed you up early."

"You're not going to talk to dad about this are you?"

"Terrell, it doesn't matter. He doesn't care, as long as you're not in trouble. So, I don't see why we should. He's only going to ask the same questions I did. Besides, I can keep a secret." Mrs. Brown replied, while she was still chopping up cheese for the lasagna.

"I just wanted to talk to him about some guy stuff, that's all."

"You like her don't you?"

"Yeah, she's okay, I wouldn't mind being her friend."

"That's all you'll better be."

"This is why I would rather talk to dad." Aldis just started laughing.

"He should be home shortly, there's not that much real estate he can sell in one day."

"I'm going to my room, I have homework to do."

Terrell runs upstairs to his room, and pulls out his phone to shoot June a quick text.

"Hey girl"   **2:30 P.M.**

....

On the other side of town June was walking out the school, and making her way to the student pick up section. Full of energy from the nap she took. When she notices her dad haven't arrived, she took a sit on the red bricks, and pulled her phone out her back pocket to respond to the loud beep. In the midst of replying to Terrells text message, she was startled by a man's voice.

"June, get in this car."

54

"Hi, to you too dad. How was your day?" June replies sarcastically.

She doesn't hesitate to jump in his all black AMG C-Class Mercedes Bens, with the black chromed out rims, and tinted windows to match. She strapped on her seat belt, as the Benz took flight.

"June don't get smart with me, I am your father not some chump on the streets." Clay replies. "Now, what's all this bullshit about you, and some nappy headed boy name Terrence? You'll skip work to have sex? What the hell is wrong with you girl?"

"It's Terrell dad, and he hasn't done anything to me. Know more than you have anyway." June whispered under her breath, but loud enough where Clay could hear her.

"What the hell does that mean?"

"Well, Dad! It means... Wait! Why am I calling you dad? Clarence or Clay, or whatever you want to be called. You don't think I've noticed how you look at me? The way you watch me as I walk by? The times I've seen you peeking in my door to watch me get dressed, or the times you staggered into the house, and you laid on my chest pretending I was my mother."

"Little girl! I almost slap the shit out of you. June, let me tell you something. You think you got something on me, you have no idea. I'm the king of that castle, and what I say goes. Besides, you most like ever portion of whatever I'm doing, because you haven't said one word to me, or your mother. So, why bring it up now?"

"That's because I love my mother you loser, and although you're a dumb punk, I will never do, or say anything to hurt my mother."

"You better watch your month little girl, before I put something in it that you just might like." Clay replies, with a blank stare, and no concern. "Which, I see you didn't mind letting some little knucklehead boy fuck the shit out of you, which I'm sure that hurt your mother's feelings. So, my little antics are nothing."

June replies with a slow attitude trying to put Clay in his place.

"I say what I want, when I want, and you may be the king of that castle, but you're not the king over me. By the way butthole, I'm still a virgin. Why you think I'm out here sleeping with any dude. Sorry, but I do have class unlike the man that my mother chose."

"I brag to differ. You see! I can have you if I please, and your mother will never know. June, what you fail to understand is that your mother loves me more than she loves you, so whatever you think, or say, she won't believe you. Let me tell you why, you're just a little whore June. You run around with these boys, giving your mother the illusion that you're this little good girl. Yeah, you're an honor student, and have a job, big deal. But, I see right through all of that good girl bullshit. Any girl, who enjoys her father taunting her, will eventually want to act on it."

June just sits in silence, no response, or reaction as if she didn't hear a word he said.

"You know what, I'm not even gon feed into your bull Clay. I will be quiet, because my revenge will come one day. As a matter of fact Clay, I will no longer call you dad. You have lost that respect, and if you hear me call you *"dad"* it's out of respect for my mother, and believe me that's it.

"Well, look who has a couple of balls today." Clay replies with laughter. "I will take you to the cleaners without a thought in my mind." Clay replied, as he softly grabs Junes thigh.

"Don't you ever touch me," says June with extreme force, as she slaps his hand away. "Will you hurry up and get me home. I have homework to do. Clay!"

"Yes, ma'am! My little sexy princess, but remember you are going to respect me. So, I will be Dad, especially if your mother is around. Do you understand? And I dare you say one word of this conversation to your mother, that ass whooping she gave you, will be nothing compared to what I'll do to you. Now, as usual, give me kisses so I can go back to work."

June could only reply, "Only in your wildest dreams, butthole." Then softly whispers "I mean dad." She then slams the car door with disgust.

This driveway, and these ten stairs are starting to be my daily walk of shame. June says to herself, as Dawn waits for her at the door.

"Hey sweetheart, how did the conversation go with your dad?"

This can't be my life. I'm only eighteen, and going through things grown women should be dealing with. I'm out of here as soon as graduation is over. I'm going to a college so far away that they will have to take a plane, and a bus ride, followed by a train to come see me.

"June!" Mrs. Avery calls.

"Yes, mother." So lost in her thoughts, she forgot her mother was speaking to her.

"How did it go?"

Can I at least put my bags down. June spoke with her eyes, but used the proper words needed not to disrespect her mother. "It went ok. Clay, I mean *"dad"* as usual yelled, and screamed, but nothing more, nothing less."

I just couldn't do it. I can't tell her, I have to spare my mother's feelings. I love her too much, and I know that conversation me and Clay had will kill her.

"I see." Mrs. Avery replies. "June, is Clay in the garage?"

"No ma'am, he's headed back to his office, he said it was some stuff he needed to catch up on."

"Hmm! Well, I guess, I can go over the new rules that will be put in order from this day forward."

They both sat at the kitchen table where June prepared herself a snack, and Mrs. Avery laid down the repercussions from Junes behavior. Mrs. Avery never even looked up from prepping dinner.

"There will be no cell phone, no driving, and no going out with your friends, no malls, no movies, or nothing else you can think of, and especially no boys.

"What else is there to do?"

"Read a book. That's what my parents told tell me, but I do got one good thing for you."

"What could possibly be good?" June asked. Waiting for her mother to say something sarcastic.

"You can go back to work, but you have to follow Bill's rules there. So, Yep! That's about all you're going to be doing for a month, maybe longer. While Miss Lady, do you have any question?"

"No, at least I have my job. Thanks mom!"

"You're welcome, now run upstairs, and do your homework."

June does as told, but not once did she believe her mom was okay.

I know something's up with Mom. She's the one keeping all these secrets about her feelings, and I still don't know why she waits up for that deadbeat."

June closed the door to her room, but opened the vent, so she could hear what was going on downstairs.

"Hey, Johnny"

"Hey, Mrs. Avery! How are you?"

"I'm fine, thanks for asking. Is Clarence in today?"

"No, ma'am! He took a personal day today."

"Oh yeah, that's right! I'm sorry Hun, I remember now. How's your mother?"

"She's good."

"Great, well you have a nice day!"

"I will, and you do the same, Mrs. Avery."

"Thanks!"

Mrs. Avery hangs up the house phone, and grabs her cell phone with a quick text to Clay.

Where are you?   **7:30 P.M.**

I know you're reading these messages you have a iPhone jackass!!!   **8:50 P.M.**

Now where is this asshole? I got his damn number, trying to play me, like I'm some kind of fool. If he running these streets again, that's his ass. I know his little skeletons. I will put him out there so fast he'll think revolution came, left, and returned again. I'm getting tired of these games.

Dawn paced back and forth for a couple minutes, as she spoke out loud to herself. She then decided to take a shower to calm her nerves. When that didn't work, it was time to clean. Although, the house was cleaner than Mr. Clean himself, she still manage to stay busy. It was now **12:24 AM**, and Clarence still hadn't made it home. So, she decided to go downstairs, and have a snack. By this time she heard the door to the garage open, and the back door shortly followed.

"Hey, Honey." Mr. Avery speaks as he staggers in the door.

"Bitch, where you have been?"

"What did I do?"

"Dude, don't play with me. I see you trying to make my hood side come out, which I'm trying to do away with. Let's not forget where I was born, and how we handle things. We don't play this shit in Pontiac, and I know you got my text messages. So, like I said. Where have you been?"

"Babe!" Is the only word Mr. Avery could mimic, and he completely disregarded her other questions.

"Clay, my patience is thin." Say's, Mrs. Avery, raising her tone.

"Don't worry about where I been. I been out, that's where." Clay says, as he runs to her arms looking for affection.

"Clay, it's **12:30 A.M.** You didn't go to work today. What the fuck is that I smell? Liquor, again! I know, I don't smell liquor on your breath? Oh! Hell, No! I know you not drinking tonight. Clarence Markel Avery, I can't believe you. We both promised to stay clean for the sake of June. It's been 17 years. Why? Why did you pick up that habit again? What are you doing to yourself?"

She was so taken back, she couldn't even cry. "I'm so disappointed in you. It's a damn shame. You a grown ass man, and has fallen off after 17 good years." Dawn just shakes her head, as walks pass Clay, and he could barely follow.

"But, honey! I just need some of that good old fashion loven." Clay says, as he tugs on her silk pink nightgown, after laughing at his own statement.

"Come on. Let's go to the room before June wakes up, and see you like this."

"Whatever." He replies, and continues to laugh.

Mrs. Avery used all her strength to drag him up the stairs, and to their bedroom. But, after so long his body was so heavy, that she couldn't do anything but let him collapse at the top of the stairwell, and her body followed shortly after.

"Forget this, you're on your own. I'm done carrying yo black ass up these stairs." Gasped Mrs. Avery as she slowly opened the door to a cold gush of wind, and the scent of a vanilla candle that burned on her nightstand.

"So!" Clay replied, as he crawled the rest of the way into the room.

He tried to catch a grip on the single love seat that was close to the door to pull his self up, but he landed face first back on the champagne carpet.

"Babe did you see that?" Still laughing as he used the nightstand for support this time, and at first pull a picture of June stared him straight in the face.

"June, June, June! Is that all we ever talk about. Damn, she must be the only person that lives in this house. I'm so sick of this little girl."

"Clay, Please Stop!"

"No! I can say what I want, when I want. And I'm saying, Yes! I know I've been with her since birth, but I wanted my own child. My child! A kid who has Clay Avery's blood running through his, or her veins. What about our baby? What about my baby, which you lost? You don't remember, do you? Today it would've been his, or her first birthday. May 15, 2015. I will never forget this date."

"Clay, please be quiet. I really don't want to relive that day."

Mrs. Avery got up from her side of the bed, and quickly stepped over Clay, who was still laying on the floor. Rushing to the bathroom with symptoms of anxiety, and her eyes full of tears. She couldn't help but touched all the cream like handles that matched her bedroom walls. Her stomach begins to bubble, and everything looked like a maze. Mrs.

Avery knew she needed a serotonin to relax her nerves before

it was too late.

"NO! You be quiet, Dawn. I can speak the truth. I can

say what's on my mind. What, you don't want little June to

hear us? Well, who gives a shit.

"No, because it hurts too bad."

"Now it hurts. Now you feel it, now you feel how I've

felt for a year."

"Clay, please just lay down, and go to bed."

"I'm going to bed, but this is complete bullshit. We

never talk about what happened to our baby, my baby. The

doctors say stress. I say bullshit. The doctors say not to

worry, it's not your fault. I say it's bullshit. How could you do

this June?" Mr. Avery slapped Junes photo, as it took flight

in the air. Given him enough room to prop his hand on the

dresser, and push his self up onto the bed."How could you

just let our baby die?"

"Clay, what the hell! Who did you just call me?"

"You know what, or who the hell I meant."

"Clay, every time you've come home drunk for the past couple of days, you've called me June, Why?"

"Dawn, I don't know what the hell you're talking about, but I'ma lay down, before it goes down!"

"Clay, I'm gon ask you one time, and one time only. Have you "EVER," before Mrs. Avery could complete her sentence she heard a small knock on the door that startled her.

"Mom, are you ok?"

"Yes, we're just fine." Clay replied.

"June, please go back to your room." Mrs. Avery said, speaking softly. "I told you to quiet down Clay, but no you had to prove your point."

"Mom!" June yells, "I'm coming in."

"June, I told you to go to your room. I will be there shortly."

"I'm not leaving this door until you do."

Mrs. Avery couldn't do anything, but make hand jesters pointed in the direction of a drunk, and oblivious Clay. Who could care less, if June was at the door, or not.

"She probably has been at the door the whole damn time."

"Yep, I sure have! Now let my mother out, loser."

"Dammit, Clay! Look what you did. Now, let me go see what's going on with our child."

Dawn scoots to the other side of the bed, pushing Clay out the way. Making a small crack in the door, she made eye contact with June.

"I'm coming June. Go to your room, I'll meet you there in a minute."

June did as told, as Mrs. Avery heard her door slam. Completely drained from the conversation she had with Clay. She had no will power for the talk, she needed to have with her daughter. Needless to say, she got fully dressed, then eased her way down the hall. She took a moment at the door to regroup, when she heard June talking to herself.

I completely understand why mom feels the way she do. Dealing with this douche bag, will drive anyone crazy. I'm glad the punk ain't my real father. It all makes better sense now. Why he hasn't truly loved me. Why he totally ignores me, why he never comes home anymore. Which, I really don't care. I'm glad he doesn't love me, I'm completely glad. I'm glad the loser ain't my father, so glad. Why would they lie to me, or hold such a secret for so long? I mean, I'm eighteen. Which, why should I care given the way he treats me. I should be glad.

June was sitting on her bed trying to hold back the tears of her pain, when her mother walked in. Not having a full understanding of the things Clay has done to her daughter. Dawn lays Junes head on her shoulders while using a Kleenex to wipe away her tears.

"Sweetheart, tell me you're okay."

"Mom, are you okay?"

"Yes! I'm just fine. Sweetheart is there something I need to know?"

"Mom, I heard Clay yelling at you tonight, are you sure you're okay?"

"June, I don't care what you heard, but don't you ever use that kind of language. You will respect him, he's still your father. So, what exactly did you hear? And you didn't answer my question. Is there something I need to know?"

"I'm sorry mom, but he's stupid. And, I heard thing's that should've been told to me years ago, but it's ok. I'm glad the poor loser ain't my real father. And, No. There's nothing."

"Please, you can tell me."

"Mom."

"Hun, there's nothing I can do until you tell me."

June was speechless. She never felt this much sympathy from her mother, and wanted to express her empathy, but couldn't get pass the fact that Clay wasn't her real father.

"We'll just leave it alone for now, and go to bed."

"No, mother! No, we are not just going to leave it alone, that's the problem."

"June, go to bed."

"Mother, why didn't you tell me Clay wasn't my real father?"

"June, Clay is your father, he raised you, didn't he?"

"Yes, ma'am, but I do not have his DNA in my blood. Like he said, but it's cool tho. I have no regrets, I'm still alive. I'm still glad he's not my father, best decision you've made."

"June!"

"Mother, I'm serious."

"Go to bed, and we will talk about this in the morning."

"Will you at least lay with me? I don't want you to go back in there with that pig."

"Yes, June! Now lay down."

"Mother!"

"What June?"

"One more question,"

"Yes June."

"He's never hit you, have he?"

That question took Dawn by surprise. Why would she ask me that? I hope I haven't put my child in an unstable environment, where she thinks I would allow abuse to take place. Dawn just shook her head, as she thought in silent before replying back."

"No! Sweetie, he's never hit me! Sweetie, I understand that you're hurt by hearing this poor news. Yes, we! No, I'll say I should've of told you from the beginning. That still doesn't take away from who Clay has been to you. Your father has his flaws, but he's still raised you. Clay has always been supportive of you, and everything you have done. He's never asked any questions. June, whatever you needed, or wanted he made sure you had. Me and his relationship, is completely different than the relationship you and him have developed. You two have a close bond, and that is something that no one should break, not even me. But, let me ask you this."

Dawn became hesitant before speaking, and decided to just be direct. "Um, has Clay every touched you? And, I mean in any way that has made you uncomfortable?"

"Mom, if you really knew him." June just shook her head. "Trust me! You would understand why I feel the way I do."

"What don't I know June? Come on dear, talk to your mother."

Dawns ear's were wide open, and she was ready to hear what her gut feeling had been telling her. She felt maybe she should've taken Clays feelings into consideration about the baby she lost, but that's something she would have to deal with on her own time. Right now she needed to know what has, or has not happened to her daughter. But, June said nothing. Her eyes did all the talking, but her lips didn't move.

Now is the time to tell her everything that he has said to me, or has made me feel. Then maybe she'll leave him.

"No mom, I have nothing to say. It's already been a terrible night."

"June if there's anything, please! I beg you to tell me."

"It's nothing mom, let's just go to bed."

Mrs. Avery waited for June to fall back asleep, as she made her way back to the room where Clay had fallen back on the floor. Stepping over him, Dawn jumped in the shower where continuous tears started to flow. Crying out loud didn't ease the pain of the heartache of what she felt her daughter was going thought. Steam filled the room before she closed her eyes in prayer.

Lord, I can only pray he's never touched my daughter. I know something happened, but I just can't place it right now. I really don't want to make false accusations. Please Lord, I ask you to open my eyes to the things I'm blind to, and brighten my spirit to the unknown.

Dawn stayed in the shower until the water grew cold. Stepping out, she wiped the mirror only to find her eyes puffy, and red. Making her way to the nightstand became a bigger task, as she once again stepped over Clay, to get her silk nightgown out her dresser. She couldn't help, but wipe more tears, as they began to fall on the back of his head. The house was completely silent, and Mrs. Avery made her way to the downstairs guest room. Where she continued to pray over her situation, asking God for more guidance, until she fell asleep.

5

Pulling up to the school, June was so thankful her mother let her drive today. A month had passed and things were finally going back to what felt like normal. As usual, she had to take some time to get herself together in the driver side window.

Here we go, back to this place. This school is so lame. I can't wait until this weekend I'm turning all the way up! It's been a month since all that stuff happened, and now I'm finally off punishment. It's on now! I still haven't fully discussed everything that happened with mom and Clay. Which they haven't taken the time to talk with me either, but at this time, I really don't care. But, at least I can go back to work. I been laid off for a while, and that hurt my pockets.

But, Bill old ugly self, go tell Mark, I couldn't return back until my punishment was over. That way, there's know additional drama between me, and my mother. Which I'm not worried, because when I see Bill, he will get some words from me. He got me up here, explaining to all my co-workers that I go to school with, what happened that night. All, because he wants to run his big mouth. Which it wasn't his place to call my mom the day I left anyway.

June's mind was getting things in order, as she walked down the hall to the cafeteria. Preparing her mind for the summer, and waving at friends.

I'm glad mom saved my job, because without it, I would be stuck at home. The tension is just too heavy there, and it's hard for me to function. So, I'm just go leave these couple of weeks in the air. I'll do as I'm told, so I can keep my GPA at a 3.9, and a 4.0 when I graduate. I won't talk to anyone, stay to myself, and leave Terrell alone. He's the reason I'm in this mess anyway. I've seen him passing in the halls, but I always fine a way to dodge him, and he's made no effort to talk to me. Not that I can tell anyway. Well, he did trap me that one day, but Vice Principle Williams stopped him before I could reply to his question.

June finally takes a seat at the lunch room table, where of course Stephanie is waiting to talk to her.

"Hey June."

"What's up Stephanie?"

"Shit, I can't call it. Waiting for the bell to ring. Girl, you would be so proud of me. I have been getting here on time, because you know I can't afford to get in no more trouble. Anyway, have you seen Terrell today?"

"No, and don't care if I do."

"Yeah, that's what your lips say, but we both know the truth."

"Stephanie, don't start with me."

"Well, there he is June, right over there."

"So!"

"Terrell," Stephanie yells.

"Girl, chill! Don't say nothing leave him alone."

"Girl, he walking this way." Stephanie replied, as if she wasn't the one who called him over.

June just sat back with no expression on her face, but her eyes said it all. This boy is sexy. Those long dreads, plump lips, those open yet slanted hazel brown eyes. I can't stand it. Then he has the nerve to have on those gray basketball shorts, and you know I'm looking for a print.

June! Get yo thoughts together. He ain't about to have you drooling. Look at those basketball legs, and those football shoulders. What am I going to do? Lord, please give me the strength to make it though the rest of the school year the way you brought me in this world, and that would be a virgin.

"Good morning ladies, how are y'all doing?"

"Hi Terrell," Stephanie replied. "What's been up withca?"

"And miss June! How are you?" Terrell extended a special greeting to June, but she didn't reply.

Here we go with that deep sexy voice. June still in a daze joined the conversation after Stephanie gave her a bump on the shoulder.

"I'm good Terrell, thanks for asking." June looked up, giving Terrell the flirty eyes of desire.

"I've called you several times throughout the weeks. Where have you been?"

"Around!"

"Yeah, ok! I see." Terrell smiles showing off all 32 of his pearly white.

Oh lord! I ain't go make it, I ain't go make it. June just replied with a smile, trying her best not to feel threatened by this fine specimen of a man in front of her. Stephanie politely pushes June out the way to get herself noticed by Terrell.

"Terrell, I asked you a question."

"What would that be Stephanie?" Terrell asked as he never took his eyes off June.

"What did you do this weekend?"

"Bye you guys" June replied, as she got up from her seat, knowing Terrell was watching.

Putting a little more bounce in her walk, so her butt will jiggle in that purple, and gold sun dress. She knew Terrell was watching her every step, but she didn't mind. It gave her the confidence she needed to feel like she can take on the world.

"Damn, girl!" Terrell yells. June smiles, and throws her hand in the air with a feeling of accomplishment.

"Terrell"

"Damn! What girl? What the hell do you want? What's so important that it couldn't wait?"

"Terrell, what's going on with you and June?"

"Is that a concern of yours Stephanie? No! It is not."

"You know what, forget it. I will just talk to you about it later, damn!"

"Yeah, you do that" Terrell replied, as they both go down the hall in different directions.

"June, wait up!" June slowed her pace down, allowing Terrell to catch up.

"Terrell, I'm mad with you!"

"Why? I haven't done anything."

"Yes, you have. You have been going around the school telling people I gave you head, and I do believe that's something, which it's called lying. Because, you know that didn't happen.

"June! I promise, I haven't told anyone. Think about it! Have you, yourself, heard anyone ask you about that night?"

"Yeah, Stephanie."

"Man! Please, don't believe nothing that girl tells you. I have not spoken one word about that night to no one, not even my boys. I didn't want you to get in anymore trouble. I didn't know the story you told your parents, and the next day when I came to school looking for you, you didn't come. When I tried to ask you, that day I trapped you in the hall. Mr. Williams stopped me."

June paused as her and Terrell stood at the side door of her classroom. Now that I think about it, no one asked me except Stephanie. How did she know, and why would she lie? That's my best friend, we tell each other everything. Looking up, she made eye contact with Terrell.

"I'll just meet you later if you want."

"I would definitely be up for that."

"No head, of course."

They both started laughing, as they know that's been said before. He then opens the door to her class as she walks in.

"Bye friend." He says, as she just smiles.

Terrell smiles, and starts to walk away before hearing his name yelled.

"Terrell!"

"Yes, Stephanie!" He replies, as if he's completely bothered. "You must work for inspector gadget, because you always know where I'm gon be, and how late I've been there. Then you pop up out of no where witcha hat on, and yo spidey senses asking questions."

"Ha Ha! What's up with us?"

"Ain't shit up with us, Stephanie."

"Oh! So, You all about June now?"

"Exactly, now leave me alone. And, another thing. How did you know me, and June were riding around? Doing whatever we damn well pleased might I add. By the way." Terrell leans in loser to Stephanie's ear. "If she did give me head, which she didn't, it ain't none of yo damn business." Terrell started walking away. "I don't even know why you are going around lying to people."

"I thought we had something special."

Terrell grabbed her by the arms, before she knew what he was going. "Stephanie, I will kick your ass, if I ever hear you say those words again."

As the halls cleared, he releases her from the locker he had her pinned up against forgetting that he was at school.

"Terrell! Damn, is it that serious?"

"Hell, yeah! It's that serious. I don't want no one to know that we're affiliated."

"We do have a child together, asshole."

"Bitch, don't you ever bring Ally into this." Terrell replies, slinging her to the other side of the empty hall. Stepping directly into her face, his true feelings showed off about what he really felt about Stephanie.

"She hasn't seen, or heard about you in almost three years, so there's no reason to start now."

"Please get your finger out of my face Terrell, and no matter what she is still our child"

"No. Correction she's my child! You can say she was your child, and that's only because you gave birth to her. But, that doesn't make you a mother. Why you always trying to bring this bullshit up at school? Stephanie, you know what!" Terrell takes a deep breath. "Please, and I do mean, please just leave me the fuck alone. I don't have time for this."

Terrell punches the locker, and starts to walk away, but Stephanie continued to chase him down. "Stephanie I can't handle your shit today. Leave me the hell alone. As a matter of fact, stay the fuck away from me from this point on. Don't call my phone, or my mothers. Don't send Ally any more of your lamn birthday cards, which we don't give to her anyway. Just leave us alone. Do you understand? And if I hear any of this from June, I promise you'll see a side of me you never seen before. She doesn't know about Ally, and we're going to keep it that way. Understood?"

Stephanie couldn't do anything but cry, and try to plead her case.

"Damn! Terrell I just wanted to know how Ally was doing. What's the harm in that? And, at some point. I will have to tell June, she is my best friend."

"Like hell you will. Stephanie if any of this gets out. I'm telling you, that's yo ass. I ain't never hit a woman, but bullshit with me if you want to. You won't live to see the next day."

Stephanie was at a complete loss for words. She couldn't do anything, but run off to the bathroom in complete despair from Terrell's feelings. She was totally oblivious to Maya, who was chasing her down, in hopes that she was okay.

Maya tried to enter the restroom, but the door appeared to be stuck. Stephanie's foot blocked the doorway from lying across the cold bathroom floor. Leaving her head rested in her arms, and her body propped to the side. Completely torn from being manhandled by Terrell, that was the only way she knew how to express herself in that meant.

"Stephanie, are you okay."

"Yes! Now please leave me alone. I'll be out in a minute."

"Okay! I'll be outside this door waiting for you. So, if you miss the bus we can walk home together."

"Okay!" Stephanie replies, trying to catch her breath.

"What was all that about Steph?"

"Absolutely nothing,"

"He had you pinned up pretty bad."

"Look, that ain't none of your fucking business. Now please just drop it."

"Fine, are you ready?"

"Yeah! We can go home now." Stephanie replied, as she opened the door still wiping tears from her face. "I missed my last class dealing with this dude. I really needed to be there."

"It's cool. I have the notes from fourth block. Which, Mrs. Reed said, she will still give an overview for the finals next week."

By this time the girls heard the sounds of the marching band practicing. There was no doubt that they would be walking home. Maya wanted to ask Stephanie more question about what happen with her and Terrell, but didn't want her to get upset again. So, she redirected the conversation to Stephanie's grades, making sure she wasn't in the zone of failing.

"You are walking Stephanie? Right!"

"Girl, I hope so! I only missed a couple days here in the last two weeks, nothing major! I had a grade point average of 2.9 on our last report card, so I should be good."

"I just didn't want you to have to go to summer school. Maybe, we can turn up this summer like we did last year. You know, it is our senior year." Maya smiled, as she noticed Stephanie slowing down on Erin street.

"Maya, I'll get at you later. I'm stopping by June's house before I go home. Thanks for walking with me, and making sure I was okay."

"Girl, you good. Get at me later, so I can give you these notes."

"I hear you." Stephanie replies as she walks up to June's gated community.

"No wonder June doesn't have a care in the world. Look at this house, it's bigger than three of my apartments put together."

Stephanie walked up the stairs, and straight through the gate. There was know request for a password, because the gate was already open. Stephaine rung the doorbell, before giving the door a light tap. Dawn peaked out the drapes, and let here in.

At first glance she noticed the marble flooring. She continued to look around given that it was her first time inside Junes house. They usually meet at the park, or at the end of the gate at the bottom of the hill.

This place is so dope. The glazed wooded stairwell, which centered the hallway, several chandeliers, and what seems to be five bedrooms upstairs. This place looks like a music video. I couldn't dream I had a place like this. Why are all my friends rich but me?" Stephanie thought, but needed to focus on what Mrs. Avery was saying.

"Hey, girl."

"Hello, Mrs. Avery. How are you doing?"

"I'm good Stephanie, how about you? Staying out of trouble I hope!"

"Yes, ma'am, as much as I can." They both started laughing. "Oh honey, I know you're a good girl. It's this June we need to be worried about." They both followed with more laughter. "How are your mom and dad?"

"Ok, I guess. They stopped by the other day to check on me." Stephanie knew she was lying, because she hadn't seen her mother in months maybe a year. And, for sure it's been three years since she seen her father last.

"Well, good! I never really understood you and your parents' relationship, but that's none of my business. I just know you're always pleasant when I'm around. But, I know you didn't come here to talk to me, so let me go get June, as if she doesn't know you're here." Mrs. Avery walked out the dining area calling June's name. "June, you have company."

June bolts down the stairs, and pulls Stephanie by the collar, through the kitchen, and out through the patio doors to the back yard.

"Bye mom." June yells as they all started laughing.

"Y'all be careful." Mrs. Avery replies, catching the loud slam of the door. Stephanie couldn't even finish her sentence of good bye before they both were outside.

"What took you so long, school been out?"

"Nothing, I was talking to Maya crazy ass. Oops! Did your mom hear me?"

"Girl no, you good! But, anyway. Maya texted me a couple minutes ago."

"Really? What she say?"

"Nothing much, just that Terrell had you pinned up to a locker about fifteen minutes before school let out. What was that all about? Is it something I need to know? Y'all both been acting crazy, and I don't like it."

"It ain't nothing to worry about. You know how crazy Terrell is."

"Yeah! I know, but that just sounded weird. So, I just had to ask, but anyway. Steph, I'm so glad next week is finals week. I'm graduating at the top of the class as valedictorian, then school is OUT". June throws her hands in the air, with a sigh of relief. "Dang, I can't wait. I just might move to Pontiac for the summer, and be with my northern family. You know they turn up! I just need to get away from this place for a little while."

"You act like you got it so bad. You living pretty good to me. Look around! What do you have to complain about? You've seen where I stay, and don't even think about moving. You're staying right here with me for the summer, we besties for life. We can rule Waco, and have these hoes hating all summer." They both started laughing getting their game plan together.

"On another note, let's clear some stuff up?"

"Yeah, what's up?" Stephanie replies knowing exactly where this conversation is going.

"You lied to me about what Terrell was going around the school saying. *"That I was given him head,"* knowing good, and well that wasn't true. Why you do me like that? Do you, and Terrell have a thing for each other, or something? Maya, said after you and Terrell was talking, you ran to the bathroom crying. So, something was said."

"Bitch, please! Trust me. Terrell and I are nothing! He can't stand my guts, that's basically what we talked about.

He's into you, and the rest was how he hates me. So, basically that was it. Nothing more, nothing less."

"You sure?"

"Yeah"

"Okay!" June replies. "I just wanted to get that cleared up, because I'm really starting to feel him. I mean, he could be the one."

"The one for what?"

"You know, the one! I've never had sex. Have you?" Stephanie just looked at June with a vague look on her face.

"Umm! I mean! I'm no virgin. I've only been with one person, and trust me the outcome was worth it, but nothing else. I'm just gon tell you this. You think these guys are for you, and they love you, but they only want one thing from you, and that's your cat. Once they get that, they're on to the next. Like you was never there. "

"Steph, who is this guy? Do you still love him? And do y'all still talk? Why didn't you tell me? Do I know him? How old were you? Does he live in Texas?

"Damn, bitch! So many questions, so little time." They both started laughing.

"All I'ma say is just be careful who you choose. You only get one chance at your first time, and it will be with you for the rest of your life. Now let's just move on, it's nothing more worth talking about. I want to enjoy my weekend, and turn up, Waco style. So! What's up?"

"Nothing!" June replied, "I can come to your house, and we kick it there if you want."

"Sounds good to me," Stephanie says. "I'll see you later."

"Okay."

Stephanie walks away with a heart full of hurt, and a brain full of anger.

"Stephanie! You sure you're ok?" June asked, as Stephanie begins to walk away.

"Yeah, I'm good."

June knew that was a complete lie. Something just doesn't seem right, but she let Stephanie continue to walk. Thinking to herself that Stephanie's expression looks just like her mothers, the night she and Clay was arguing about her. June just sat there as Stephanie walked down the street. Still in disbelief that Stephanie wasn't a virgin.

I can tell she has a lot on her mind, but I never thought that sex was one. I mean, that's all these girls talk about now days. How they had an orgasm, how they gave, or got some head, and that sex was the best thing that they experienced. But, Stephanie seems completely bothered by it. Maybe I need to rethink my position about sex, and just wait until I'm married. That way, I know the man that I'm with, will not be going anywhere. Dang! Maybe I should've offered her a ride, she does live a pretty good ways away."

Stephanie didn't even look back. She was so deep in her thoughts, she didn't even take the distance of the walk to heart.

I will pay Terrell back one day. Hell, the brown family in general, they have caused me so much pain not to feel my wrath. Now, I have to sit here and be friends with June, but why? We have nothing in common. She's a spoiled brat, with lack of appreciation for what she has. That's probably why Terrell likes her. Man! How can one man get on your nerves so much, but you still have love for him. I'ma have to find a way to shake both of them, before I lose my damn mind.

By the time Stephanie got home it was after seven. She made a couple stops at the convent store, but walked most of her anger off along the way. After a hot shower, and a hot pocket for dinner, she headed to the rooftop of her building where she went for peace.

6

"Hey, honey!"

"Hi, Ma. How is your day going? Where is Ally?"

"She's upstairs taking a nap. How are things going with you Terrell. It seems like we haven't talked in a while? What's up son, spill it." Aldis walks over to Terrell, and sits beside him to dip in her son's life for a minute.

"Mom, it's Stephanie again. She's really getting under my skin. Today at school, we got into a big altercation about Ally. She talks about how she needs to be in Ally's life. Mom, I straight up told her, get the heck on. Well, in so many words. Then, she wants to bring up this one girl we both are mutual friends with. Asking me what's up with our relationship. I'm like that's none of yo business. Man a swear, she just won't leave me alone."

"June! Right?"

"Yeah! How did you know?"

"That doesn't matter, just know that I know. I'm your mom, and we know these things." They both smiled, knowing she ease drop on his conversations, when he's home.

"Well anyway, back to Stephanie. Mom, she keeps starting this big thing about how she wants to spend more time with Ally. How we never bring her around, and that I need to basically give us a chance as a family. I was so pissed off mother. I really wanted to hit her, but I remembered what you told me. Never put my hands on a female. I told her, look we at school, I don't have time for this, and I'm sure someone heard us. So, I just left the situation alone. I was just all around pissed that she was even talking to me. I couldn't do nothing but walk away."

"Terrell that's none of her business what Ally is doing, or what she's up to. This is the very reason we got her to sign that release waiver, so that way she can't ask no questions."

"So mom, while we're talking. What's the whole story? I mean, me and Stephanie were cool. She was my ace, but then when she got pregnant things went completely downhill. And, why did she have to sign her rights over? We both were young, unmarried, and was new to parenthood. One day I went to go see her, and her parents put her out of their house. The next day at school, all our friends said she no longer went to the school. I went back to her parents house, and when I asked her mother what was going on. She said, she got her an apartment across town. I'm just completely confused about the whole situation.

During the whole process I was missing in action, and really couldn't take in the fact that I was about to merge into fatherhood. Especially, at such a young age. I mean, I'm completely glad it happened, because Ally is my life. I wouldn't be anything, or grind as hard to make my career goals complete without her. It's just some stuff I don't understand."

"Hun! It's a lot we as your parents felt neither you nor Stephanie would understand at your age. Well, let me just set the story straight. When Stephanie found out she was pregnant, she came to my office completely distraught. When she told me why I tested her all ways possible, and of course the test can back positive. We both broke down crying out of disbelief. She was so hurt that she didn't want to keep Ally, but I informed her that it was for the best. I then told her. The next big thing was to tell her parents, and then we would go from there. Trust me son, as a parent that's the last thing you want to hear from a friend is that your child is pregnant. But, of course, when she told her parents, and like me, they were saddened. We all met again to figure out what was best for the situation.

Her parents were so disgusted with this pregnancy that they wanted to abort the baby as well, and that's when me and your father took over. The Taylors and I agreed that Stephanie would carry Ally full term, and we would take on the responsibilities of caring for the baby. I felt that was the best decision given the fact that our family doesn't believe in premarital sex, but since that leisure was broken. I definitely wasn't about to interfere with God's plan, and abort the baby. They agreed under the conditions that Stephanie would sign her rights over without any interference in the future. I believe they were looking out for her future, but I'm sure she doesn't feel that way."

"Mom not to cut you off, but where was Stephanie throughout this?"

"Terrell, her parents wouldn't allow her to have a say so if she wanted to. I'm sure at some point she put up a fight to keep Ally for herself, but maybe that's why she may seem a little bitter, or resentful about talking about Ally unless she's talking to you. It still hurts for me to talk about it at times, so I can only imagine how she feels. This is the very reason why we don't talk about it often. You see son, sometimes you have to understand that protection is always the best way to go when having sex. Abstinence is an even better way, but always know Terrell you will never be the blamed for any of this. I just want you to be careful so things like this won't happen to you in your lifetime.

So, please! Take it easy on Stephanie, because she only wants to be loved Terrell. I mean.. She's a good girl, but she just lost her way in all this.

You had a support system, and she really didn't. Just think, you left her, her parents abandoned her, and to top everything a child she carried for nine months was taken away. Hell, that would traumatize anyone. Nevertheless, we offered her counseling, but she refused to take it. Then I personally offered to take her to some private sessions, like I took you, but she said she was fine. She didn't want me in her life anymore, and that was the end of that. She made contact with me every now and then, but nothing worth talking about."

"Wow! I guess I owe Stephanie an apology, if not more. I never understood what she went through. I just know how I felt, and I never applied it to her feelings. I'm glad we had this talk. You really helped me to understand, and cleared the air on the whole situation. Especially from Stephanie's point of view. If you don't mind, I'm going over to Stephanie's house to do the same there. Kiss Ally for me, mother! I'll be back shortly."

"Okay, son. Please be careful."

7

Terrell jumped in his car with no hesitation. "Damn! I can't believe all that happened with Stephanie, and our child. This whole situation is too messed up. I guess I could've taken her feelings into consideration. But, I'ma drive over here, and just clear the air. I can at least, let her know that I understand where she's coming from, and what she's been through.

After a couple of blocks of riding around. Terrell turns on Pike street. I'm on third and ninth, but this can't be it. Which I've only been over here once, maybe twice, and it looked way better than this.

There is trash everywhere, trees down, abandoned cars, and cardboard windows everywhere. I'm so glad we took Ally. I wouldn't want my child raised over here. It's bad enough her mother has to live in these conditions. Damn, this ain't nothing but the projects. Let me get this over with as soon as possible. Last I remember she lived in the Hollow Way Apartments set D, on the 12th floor apt# 16. I've made several circles so it must be the next set over, cause I don't see set D.

After circling the block a couple times he rode through one final time before making his way to her section. He then parked, and walked up the indoor stairway.

Stephanie was out on the roof top enjoying the night air, and the peaceful beginning of summer. When she saw Terrell pull up.

Omg! What is he doing here? Why would Terrell be here? Stephanie, calm down, and let's play this game well.

The door to the rooftop slowly swings open five minutes later, but Stephanie know exactly who it was.

"It's such a beautiful night. Full moon, wind blowing, and freshly cut grass. You know how I like that." Stephanie slowly turns around with curiosity, and seduction

"Hey, Steph! And yes, I know how you like the night life."

"You remember how we us to lie out in the grass, and just kick it on nights like this? You know, when we were cool."

"Yeah, I know Stephanie. That's one of the reasons I'm here. How did you know it was me by the way?"

"Well, I seen you circling the blocks looking lost, and then you made your way to the back lot. Who else are you coming to see other than me?" With a slight smile on his face Terrell laughed.

"I could've been coming to see my new girl."

"Nah, not in this area. You don't date people on this end of town." Terrell just grinned, and began to emasculate his authority.

"Stephanie! Come here, move a little closer. I really want to talk to you about something very important."

Oh shit! My hearts racing. Stephaine thought, and moved closer.

"I really don't know where to start, but I do want to clear the air about some things."

"What do you want to talk to me about Terrell? You know, since you hate my guts."

They both stared out into the night lights, that overlooked the roof tops atmosphere. It gave the illusion of a full cities night with lots of lights, and heavy traffic. It was nothing short of breathtaking. The scenery helped calm Terrell nerves, and he was able to talk to Stephanie with a clear mind.

"Stephanie, listen! For real. I'm very sorry for how our conversation went at school this week. I spoke to my mother about this thing with Ally, and she told me how the whole situation went down. So, I really just wanted to apologize."

"What the fuck are you talking about Terrell? What did your mother tell you?" Anger admittedly took over Stephanie, and aggression filled her body.

"See, this is the very reason I don't talk to you Stephanie. You instantly get an attitude."

"That's just a touchy subject Terrell, but I'm willing to listen."

Stephanie just started shaking her head as Terrell begins to deliver the information that his mother provided to him.

"Stephanie my mother told me the true story on how, and why Ally is with us. What's the harm in that"

"Really, Terrell. And, whose story was told?"

"What you mean whose story did she tell? The true story Stephanie"

"No! She didn't tell the true story. She told their story."

"What does that mean? See, I knew by coming over here it would be some bullshit."

"No! The bullshit is, how y'all think because y'all got a little money, the brown family can treat people any kind of way they want to.

"How has my family treated you Stephanie? The only thing we did was try to resolve this fucked up situation with Ally." Stephanie just started walking away, but Terrell followed behind her, pulling at her arm for answers.

"Hell, No! Stephanie, now is the time to tell your side of the story."

"Terrell, Ally is your fathers. There I said it." Stephanie just broke down crying, falling to her knees.

"Fuck outta here with yo lies. Stephanie, what did you say? No! Get up! Get the hell up. What did you say? Ally! Ally, ain't mine? Whose is she then? Who the fuck is her father?" Terrell dropped Stephanie, and started pacing back and forth. "No, No! You trying to pull me into your psychotic world, and that's not about to happen. Get up!" Terrell pulls Stephanie up to her feet with one hand, and a risk jerk. "Stephanie, that's one thing you ain't gon do. You will not be little me, and my child." Terrell releases Stephanie yet again, making her feet stumble and fall back to the ground.

"She's my child to Terrell."

"Don't tell me anything else, but who's the father."

"Terrell I already told you, and it doesn't matter."

"Yes hell it does! I need to know who the father of my child is."

At this point, Terrell is right back in Stephanie's personal space, demanding answers. With both hands holding her arms, Stephanie couldn't do anything, but look him in the eye's. Stephanie, then asked to be released from his painful grip, and tried to hold herself up.

"Terrell, please let my arm go."

"No! Not until you tell me who the father is. Tell me one more time, cause it damn sure ain't my father."

"Terrell I'm sorry, but she's your fathers." Stephanie still overwhelmed with tears, and a side of relief from finally getting that off her chest. She still had a full heartache of pain, knowing she was the one who told Terrell the truth.

"What? Stephanie. What did you just say? Who? My father, my fucking father." Terrell beat his chest repeatedly trying to soften the pain of what has to be lyes.

"Bye! Stephanie. Now! I see, you've gone too far. You'll do anything for attention. That's just the wrong attention. My father! Daryl Darnell Brown, DD, Darnell. Come on Stephanie. Better yet, you told me I was the only one you ever been with."

"You are Terrell. You're the one that I agreed to. Your father raped me."

There was no turning back now, and Stephanie's eyes were full of rage, anger, and revenge. Her arms were red from Terrells forceful hands, and there was no life left in her chest from crying.

Terrell broke down with laughter and tears. "Rape Stephanie? He raped you?"

"Yes, Terrell. Please believe me."

"Why should I? You're such a liar."

"Why would I lie, Terrell?"

"Why wouldn't you lie? Let's see, you told June I told the whole school, she gave me head. I believe that's a lie, and other things Stephanie. Let's not forget I was your roll dog. I know how your scheming ass works. So, it's the same reason you're lying about this. To get things your way."

"Terrell this is too serious to lie about. Your mother signed the papers for Ally to be under her care not me. Yes, I'll agree that my parents put me out, and into this apartment. But, it was because they didn't want all their friends to know that their sixteen year old daughter was not only pregnant, but pregnant by a black man. I was so hurt and depressed, I couldn't make any decisions on how I really felt about the pregnancy. I was still overwhelmed by what your father did to me that night. I just completely lost it, and from that point on my life went down hill.

Terrell you know I've never really met your father. I've always known your mother, so he was a fresh face to me. Drinks were had, and I was trying to leave to go home, he got a room, and then took advantage of me. I never told anyone, because I didn't think no one would believe me. A month later me and you hooked up. I was two months when I found out I was pregnant, I didn't want to tell you until I know for sure who the father was. Your mother took on my case, and told me to wait until we got the results back."

"Wait! You weren't old enough to drink at a bar Stephanie, let alone get in one that server's alcohol." Terrell interrupted her before she could reply. "So my mother knew from the beginning?"

"Yes! Terrell, she knew. I didn't want to ruin your life with all this bullshit. So, I never told you, and by the way a fake ID is everything in this town."

Terrell and Stephanie was still both face to face as he stood by the central air unit, and she stood a couple feet away from him, but close enough to look him square in the eye.

"To make things worse Terrell. You started brushing me off like I was nothing to you. Especially, when June came into town. I know I'm not as attractive as June, but that doesn't mean I don't have my shit together.

Yeah! I'm a little ghetto, a plus size white chick, with a slick tongue, but you said that's what you liked about me. You said you like looking into my hazel blue eyes, and that they gave you the feeling of looking at earth close up. That I was the first white girl you seen with full lips, and they were all you needed to help you make it through the night. You liked the fact that I had hips, and couldn't dream to reach five and a half feet. I remember when you use to call me short stop, Terrell. I remember when I was your scapegoat, and that we always kept it one hundred with each other."

Stephanie completely in tears moved closer to Terrell looking for that long lost affection she always wanted from him. She lowered her voice to make things more sentimental, and soften the pain.

"I've always kept those things at heart Terrell, and always had your back for that. And, if you can only understand, I'm just tired of being treated unfairly at this point. I'm tired of no one taking my feelings into consideration. I'm tired of pretending that none of this shit happened. I've been walking around for so long, as if I have a normal life, and I don't!"

Stephanie begins to understand the real pain of her life, and that's not being a mother to the daughter that she birthed.

"I want to see my daughter Terrell. I want to be in her life. I want to have a hand at raising her, holding her, telling her I love her each day. You know the things you experience every day. I want daughter and mother dates. I want us to play at the park, go to movies, have princess parties. Do all the things that mothers, and daughters do. Go and get our nails done. Do you know how it feels to deal with this life I'm living, Terrell? To be a mother who has nothing to do with her child."

Standing with a blank look on his face, and trying to absorb how true this information was, Terrell didn't even reply.

"Terrell!" Stephanie looks him square in his puffy red eyes, snaps her fingers, and clap her hands until he looks up. "Will you please understand where I'm coming from. Getting up every morning knowing you've been raped, by the father of the man that you're in love with. Having a daughter that you've only held, and seen once. Seeing the man that you love, flirting, and trying to date a girl you have to pretend to be friends with. Why? I'll tell you why. All so you can be close to the man that you adore."

The silence grew for a second, and they both were lost in resentment.

Damn! What has my life come to? This can't be normal? This can't be the life God intended for me. You wouldn't understand my pain Terrell. You were raised with a silver spoon in your mouth. You have parents that give a damn where your life is going, and how it would end. Me on the other hand, I wasn't so fortunate. You see where I live. My parents put me in this apartment out of shame Terrell. Shame! Not to help me grow into adulthood, but because of their own self morals. They didn't love, or support me. Never gave me the feeling of understanding, or comfort. They only made my depression worse with their abandonment. To add insult to injury. I have to work while still in school, and pay my own bills without any help. I could've taken the easy route, and dropped out, but I didn't. I just wanted a better life for myself, and what could've been our family. This is not something an eighteen year old should be dealing with. My biggest concern should be what I'm wearing to prom, and not if my power bill will be paid on time. No one understands my struggle."

Terrell just looked up from the central air unit he was sitting on. Jumped to his feet, and started walking to the door.

"Terrell, please talk to me."

"About what Stephaine? You just told me the worse news of my spoiled little life, and you want me to continue to talk to you. I'm doing my best not to jump off this roof, and take you with me. I'm hurt too. Can you understand that? Do you understand my feeling at this point?"

Aggression filled the air, and it was in Terrells plans to see that his feelings got taken care of. "You talk about how damn great my life is. Did you really hear what you told me? My father raped you Stephanie. I have a daughter who's actually my sister. How does that sound? I don't know these people I've been living with for eighteen years."

Terrell couldn't get a hold of his feelings in any longer, and at this point life was worth given up on. "What man touches a woman without their permission? Why am I even sitting here talking to you about this. When I can go home, and handle this myself. I can't believe this shit!"

Pacing back and forth, Terrell begins to repeat, why with long sighs, and tears.

"My Ally, the love of my life, ain't my daughter. She's not my child. Why would you do this to me?" Terrell dropped to his knees in a praying position, and released his hurt with more tears. "Where does my life go from here?" Terrell asked as he looked up to the sky, but got no answer. "I have to go Stephanie I need answers." He gets up on his feet, and head for the door.

"Wait! Where are you going? What's your plan?"

"I don't know. I have no plans, but I do know my daughter won't be raised around those insensitive people. I can't believe this shit, she's not my daughter. She's not my fucking daughter." His anger has turned into rage, and uncontrollable fury. "They are going to pay for this bullshit. They dragged me in their low down scandal, as if I had no feelings of my own, or like I would never find out."

"Terrell, please calm down, and let's think things through."

"Calm down! Really? You want me to calm down! How the hell am I suppose to do that? Am I supposed to just act as if none of this happened? Like you have! Am I supposed to sweep this under the rug? Hell, no! My questions will be answered, one way, or another. So, I'm with you on getting revenge, but I'm not waiting."

"Terrell, we have to handle this carefully. So, my plan will follow through, and all our lives will be better."

Terrell stood with his hand on the door hand as he waited to hear her plan. "What's your plan?

"Come here, and I'll tell you." Terrell replied to the jester by grabbing her hand, and a kissing her on the forehead.

"Thank you Stephanie, in all realness. I'm glad you told me, but I have to go." Terrell kneeled down, and kissed Stephanie again.

"No! We can't! I can't, and I don't want your sympathy."

"Stephanie, please! I need this."

"It's been way too long. I don't know if this is the right timing." Terrell just completely ignored her, and removed his shirt.

"Right here? Right now?" Stephanie asked, knowing it was bad timing, but she didn't want him to stop

"Shut the hell up, and let me enjoy you." Terrell said after backing away. "That's if I'm not overstepping my boundaries." She just smiled.

He then leads Stephanie to the blanket she was sitting on before he got there. He slowly kissed her neck, and reached under her shirt to feel for her bra. Her undergarment popped off with ease, and he sucked each tittie like a new born child. Stephanie could only reply by throwing her head back.

"Lay down" Terrell said, and she followed orders. She kept her feet planted on the floor, and her knees in the air. Terrell lowered his position, and slowly raised her skirt. Stephanie was completely glad she went commando, as Terrell begins to man handle her clitoris.

"Terrell please wait! Wait one second, do you know what you're doing."

"You'll find out soon," he says as he comes up for air.

"Oh shit, I'm about to cum." Stephanie screams from the pit of her stomach, and Terrell just smiled, as he inserts the pure strength of his erection in her vagina. An explosion of liquid ran down Stephanie's lower buttocks as she widened her legs for more.

"Damn! Terrell, warn me next time." She says as her body calms down from her climax. They both started laughing as he continued with each stroke.

"You want me to stop?" Terrell asked, with the understanding that she would say no. Her body came to its peak again, and with each quiver she became more relaxed. She then rolled over in order to take control. "Damn, girl!" Terrell replied. Stephanie just smiled, and straddles him like a horse.

"Terrell!" Stephanie calls out, as she pats him on the chest coming to her senses.

"We need protection! You don't have any condoms?"

"It's too late for that. So, be quiet, stop thinking, and keep making my dick wet."

Once again, Stephanie followed orders, and Terrell cups her breast, and they both continue's to enjoy the moment. After releasing her energy again, she pulls off, lower her position, and swallows his manhood. All Terrell could do was let out a loud moan.

"Damn, girl! What the hell was I thinking leaving yo ass? I forgot how good yo sex is."

Stephanie just smiled with her mouth full of Terrell.

"What are y'all doing?"

Terrell looked up, startled. While Stephanie pulled his jimmy out her mouth.

"June" was all he could say as the door slammed.

8

Standing behind the closed doors, June stood in shock. She could barely walk with what little life she had left in her body. She was current that she just walked into a dream. But, after standing for a couple minutes, each stairwell door busted open from her making an exit.

That must have been somebody else I saw. It had to be someone else, because Terrell hates Stephanie. He doesn't even like to look her way, and from what she said he doesn't like her. So, I'm almost sure they are not on this dusty rooftop having sex. I know, I know they're not. It couldn't of been. You know what, I'ma just keep walking before I go postal. I am so pissed off right now, I can scream. I should go back up there, and put there these hands on her ugly self.

June slowed down to be sure it was her name she heard before making her way completely down the 10th floor stairwell.

"June, wait!" Stephanie yells several times, but it appears too late. She then bogarts her way to the door, grabbing her clothes, and throw them on at the same time.

"June, please wait! I didn't want you to find out this way."

June pause in her tracks. She gave Stephanie a chance to catch up, and bitch slapped her square in the face.

"Have you lost your damn mind? It's not what it looks like."

"What it looks like! Are you serious right now? You just slept with my man."

"Last I just checked, I was just sucking his dick, but sleeping together, no."

June exchanged no words, and punched Stephanie in the nose.

"Bitch!" Stephaine yelled, as June plowed on top of her.

Blow after blow was passed until the 10th floor stairs got the best of them. The name calling, heavy breathing, and bumping into doors caused the neighbors to come out. One neighbor tried to break up the fight, while others held her back so they could record the uproar for their social media page. Pushing people out the way, Terrell made his way through the crowd to break up the brawl.

"How could you Terrell?" June yelled, as he held her up against the wall. Stephanie picked herself up off the floor, and wiped blood from her nose.

"This bitch got me fucked up."

"And I will continue to," June replies, as she catches her breath..

"Well, do it bitch! I'm waiting, and will be."

"Do you see your face? I have!"

Terrell reaches his hands out in forgiveness.

"Listen June. Let me explain."

"Terrell, fuck you, and the fat bitch you rode on."

June took the 8th floor elevator to the ground floor, and ran to the car sobbing.

"Damn! Terrell, what the hell just happened?" Replied, Stephanie.

"I fucked up my future, that's what just happened. Dealing with yo ass. FUCK he yells, knowing he won't be able to get out of this one easy.

Stephanie's neighbors still were poking their heads out the window, while others returned back in their doors.

"What the fuck are y'all looking at?" She cried out, as she walks back up to the 12th floor, and back in her own apartment.

Terrell just walked the flight of stairs thinking about everything that happened.

This shit got out of hand too quick. It's 12 O'clock. June and Stephanie just got into an all around brawl. I fucked

Stephanie. Which, I promised myself, it would never happen again. Now, I have to find June. I don't know if she drove, or walked. But, I have to find her. Man! It's like every time I'm around Stephanie, my life goes downhill. But, she's so fun, and feisty, you can't help but want her around. At the same time, she's too much drama. Then there's June. She's hella fine, has a good future, life goals on point, and knows how to get there. I never got a chance to take her out, one on one, but I'm sure she's fun too. And, she'll be good for Ally. Shit! Ally, let me go get my child.

Terrell made his way to his car, and just breaks down in tears. Barley putting the car in reverse, or his seat belt on he spends off around the corner.. He picks up speed from 45 to 65, and heads in the direction of his house.

"DD got me fucked up if he thinks I'ma let this one roll off my chest."

His speed increases from 65 to 85. He barely makes the turn on 191 Simmons Ave, as he manages to keep 70mph when he rams into the garage door. Mrs. Brown jumps up out the chair she was resting in, and Darnell runs down the stairs from hearing the loud boom.

"Did you hear that honey?"

"Yeah, sweetheart! Let me see what the hell is going on," Mr. Brown replies, as he swings the door open. Mrs. Brown runs out the door, knowing it was Terrell from her peeking out the mini blinds.

"Oh my goodness! Oh lord! What happen? Terrell baby are you okay?" Mrs. Brown runs to her son's aid while he gets out the car.

"Ma, please move out my way." Terrell pushed his mother to the side, and stepped face to face with his father, who was watching his reckless behavior.

"Yo! Did you fuck Stephanie!" Mrs. Brown, head drops, as her hands covered her mouth.

"Son, what are you talking about?"

"You know what the hell I'm talking about." Pointing his hands directly in his father's face. "Did you fuck my girl Stephanie?"

"Son, calm yo ass down, and let me explain." Terrell punches his father square in the gut.

"Wit yo bitch ass, that's all I needed to know." Mr. Brown couldn't do nothing, but charge directly into Terrell's lower abdomen causing Terrell's body to slam to the ground.

"Son, what the hell has gotten into you? Now, calm the fuck down before this gets too out of control." Terrell jumps up completely in defense mode. Elbows his father in the chest, followed by a choke holds.

"Son, let me go." Darnell yells, as he punches him in the side rib.

"Hold on! Just Hold on," Mrs. Brown cries out. "Boys, we are better than this. You don't have to do this. Please break it up. Please! Break it up right now! Terrel, please! That's your father for goodness sake." Mrs. Brown, and a neighbor pull Terrell off of Mr. Brown.

"Son, get a fucking grip." He yells as he catches his breath. "And what the hell are y'all looking at, get back in y'all houses."

"Man! Fuck this shit." Terrell jumps back in his car, and starts pulling back and forth until his car is released from the garage. Mrs. Brown runs to the window to try to make peace of the situation.

"Please! Terrell! Please, let's just go in the house and talk this out before someone calls the cops, if they already haven't."

"Ma, I'm coming back for my daughter." Terrell says, and pulls off with no regret, or concern for his mothers' feelings.

"Just listen to me."

Dust flies, and tears off. There's no anguish to Mrs. Browns guilt, and the lies she held in for many years was now revealed. Mr. Brown walks back in the house, and plops down in his recliner.

"What the hell Aldis? How did he find out? Who told him? Do you realize I just got in a damn fight with my son? My son Aldis!" He screams.

Mrs. Brown runs and gets her first-aid kit to bandage her husbands bloody scars.

"We talked earlier, honey. And…" Before she could finish her sentence Mr. Brown was on his feet.

"You told him didn't you? I should beat yo ass. How dare you? Me and Terrell had that father and son bond, and you broke it. We agreed, that if nothing else, that was to never be shared, and you told the boy."

"Well, it ain't like you never hit me before." Was all she could say.

"Now you know that was our past, and you still bringing up old shit. Just like this thing that happened with Stephanie. Now, I have to get things back right with my son."

Darnell just kept pacing the floor, and trying to bandage his own wounds, as more anger set in.

"Darnell it doesn't make a difference who told him. Sooner, or later he would have found out the truth. Maybe if we were truthful from the beginning, and we talked to him, we wouldn't be in the place we are right now.

"So, now you a nurse, and a psychologist?"

"No, but I do know the truth is always better than a lie."

"Man! I still can't believe you told him. He needed to hear my truth, there's no telling what this girl has told him"

"I told him the filtered version. Just like we always told everyone else, and if you would take my class on how to keep your dick in your pants, we wouldn't be in this predicament anyway."

"Well, I didn't!" Mr. Brown yells, as he walks up the stairs, and slams the bedroom door.

Mrs. Brown just stayed put with her head rested on their custom made marble table. She couldn't help but cry, and think of how she could resolve this situation. Moments later she jumps up, and heads for the door.

Like hell, if I'm going to sit here squalling, it ain't go help nothing.

On the hunt for her keys, her phone beeps, and the alarm goes off.

Not work, please not at a time like this. Looking down at her phone completely dumbfounded to the unknown number. After glancing at the message, she then knew who it was from.

Why is Terrell's friend texting me? And, how did this crazy girl, get my number. That's right, I completely forgot that I told her she could call me anytime." Aldis fully opens the text that reads:

Hi, Mrs. Brown this is June! I hope I didn't wake, or scare you from this late night text, but If Terrell is home, I really need to speak to him, it is very important to me, and he hasn't

answered his phone. Sorry again if I woke you.
12:40 A.M.

Hi, June! This is Mrs. Brown. No, ma'am! You didn't wake
me, and I appreciate the concern. I am currently on the hunt
for Terrell, so if you know any of his whereabouts I would
really appreciate your help.
12:45 A.M.

Oh! Hi Mrs. Brown, I hope everything is ok. Last I saw Terrell
we both left Stephanie's house in a heated argument. I thought
he was going home. He flew pass me like 30-45 mins ago. I'm
over here in Bills plaza waiting for my cousin, but if I see him I
will definitely keep you informed.
12:47 A.M.

Ok dear! You said 30-45mins ago? And I will definitely do the
same. Be safe dear, and if your mother doesn't know where
you are, please inform her. We get worried at this hour.
1:00 A.M.

Yes, ma'am! To both questions
1:00 A.M.

K, Headed that way.
1:01 A.M.

Aldis slides her iPhone 6s in her Chanel purse, and heads out
to find her son.

9

My own father is a rapist. How dare he call his self raising me as a man. From the looks of it, he wasn't raised right himself? I just can't believe Ally is not my daughter. My baby girl. I love her with every fiber in my bones. She is the only human being that has my heart, and soul. Why would they do this to me? Why would they lead me to believe that she was my daughter, and knowing it wasn't true? I have got to finish this.

Terrell continues to sob. "Lord, if you hear me, help!" He spoke out loud. Picking up more speed, he notices Ricks 24 hour pond. Admittedly, he punches gas flies over dead man's bridge, and pulls the U-turn.

"Hell yeah! I got something for Darnell's ass."
Pulling in slowly, Terrell backs in, and parks at the end of the
parking lot, so his car is out of sight.

"Rick, what's up man!"

"Nothing much dude." The two slap hands to seal the
greeting.

"Damn! You good fam?" Rick replied, seeing how
bad Terrell's face looked.

"Yeah, man! I just had a fucked up night, but you
still got that 9?"

"Oh, yeah! It's in, but I'm sorry my dude! How you
looking right now, hell naw fam! I can't sell this to you."

"Come on man! I swear, it's only for my protection."

"Nah! Terrell, what's really going on?" Terrell
wanted to explain his problem to his long time friend, but it
was just too much in one night.

"Rick! Man, I promise, I'm good."

"You sure dude?" Rick replies, with concern.

"Fashow!" Terrell replied, knowing damn well his life was going downhill, and fast. "So, we good on that 9, or what?"

"I'ma sell it to you, but I need some information, and a promise you ain't gon do nothing stupid."

"I got you, fam."

Rick steps to the back, to draw up the paperwork, and Terrell looks down at his phone with continued calls from his mother, and Stephanie. He looks up when Rick asked him for his signature, and his total of 150.00 plus a 35.00 fee for his permit. Terrell pulls out his Visa card, and Rick quickly informs him that credit cards are not accepted for that kind of purchase.

"Man, you know I only accept cash on guns, but I tell you what. Since I know you, and the fam. I'll accept your card this time."

Rick then asks Terrell how his parents were doing, trying to start small talk. He had know clue he was adding fuel to the fire. Terrell just stares into space with a late reaction "they're good," as he grabs his paperwork, and shake Ricks hand.

"You all set to go, T. Please, handle this with care, bruh. It's not the gun that kills people, it's the people who choose to carry in anger, who causes harm."

"I hear ya." Terrell replied

"Real rap."

Terrell just nods his head, re-shakes Rick's hand, and smiles knowing his intentions. Jumping back in his damaged Corolla, he headed back in the same direction he came from. Leaving behind black burned tire tracts from when he peeled out. Getting his thoughts together on how he was going to carry out his revenge, he looked out the window to a girl walking in Bills Plaza.

Damn, that looks like June! Oh, hell naw! It's 1:45. That's way too late for her to be out here, her mother would kill her.

Terrell pulls out his phone to give her a quick text, to only notice he has a missed call from her. The phone rings twice before she answers.

"June, I am so sorry. So sorry.

"Terrell, today was just out of control."

"I know, and trust me things wasn't suppose to happen the way they did. Was that you I just saw walking the streets?"

"Yeah, probably. I'm staying the night with one of my cousins. We are at the gas station now, getting snacks for the movies we about to watch. I'm outside just piddling around until she gets done talking to her boyfriend. Needless to say, worrying about you. If you really want to know."

June just smiles, knowing she's trying to be flirty, so he can ask if he could join.

"Oh, really?"

"Well of course Terrell. I talked to your mother about an hour ago, and she seems very worried about you." Thirty seconds pass. "Hello! Terrell did you hear me? Terrell!" June didn't get an answer, and couldn't hear anything, but the dial tone.

Did he hang up on me? Let me call him right back. But, when she does, she gets no answer. I'm getting scared. June says to herself until her phone rings.

"Terrell, you had me worried. You must have been in a bad spot."

"Yeah! I was," Terrell reply. "I'm kind of in a rush to get home, and crossing dead man's..." the phone just drops to the dial tone again.

"What the heck! Not, again." June yells. "He really needs to get a new phone if that one keeps dropping."

Time passed, and no response. June tries to call him again, but she keeps getting the busy signal. She runs into the store, and yells to her cousin that she had to go, and began to run out the door. Her phone rings, and she instantly picked up.

"Boy! You scared me."

"Excuse me? This is Mrs. Brown, and I've been riding these roads for about an hour, and haven't seen Terrell. I spoke with Stephanie, and she told me everything that went down today. So, please tell me you've spoken to him. At least, since our last phone conversation. I'm completely worried, and about to call the police."

"Yes, ma'am! I spoke with him, and I think he's crossed dead man's bridge right now. That's why his phone keeps dropping, so when he calls me back, I'll tell him to call you."

"Okay! I'm headed that way, and please call me if you hear from him again."

Mrs. Brown hangs up the phone, then pulls a U-turn, and floors it in the opposite direction. Please! Lord, let my son be ok. This bridge is highly dangerous, and he needs your hand for his safety, especially how dark it is over there. Mrs. Brown says a quick prayer than answers her phone.

"June! Please tell me some good news."

June is completely distraught, and could barely talk. Mrs. Brown could only hear her say, he's over.

"He's what? June! I couldn't hear it all. What did you say?" June tried to repeat herself, but it just gets worse. But, by then Mrs. Brown was topping the hill, and making her way around the corner.

The streets were dark, and quiet. You could only see the reflection from the corner store lighting, which was on the next block over. The only additional lighting came from Terrells headlights, that barely peeked over the hill. Before Mrs. Brown pulled up. Her motherly intuition told her what happened, but she was still holding on to her prayer. Slowly driving around the corner, her car was still rolling in neutral from her not putting it fully in park. Once putting her car in the right gear, she sees what appears to be June climbing out of the ditch. Not being able to contain herself, Mrs. Brown runs to June screaming.

"No, No! He's ok! He has to be, I prayed! I prayed June, he's Okay." June just points down the hill where Terrell is, and continues to cry. "Okay, Aldis. Get it together."

Mrs. Brown immediately turns her doctor hat on, and, handled the situation before she loses full control.

"June, did you touch anything?" June couldn't answer, and only had a look of desperation on her face. "June I'm going to need you to get it together, if we want things to be okay. Now! Did you touch anything?" June replied quickly.

"No, ma'am, I just, I mean, the car. The car is on top of him, and I couldn't, I just couldn't see him."

"Okay, honey, calm down. Take my phone. Go to the top of the hill, where there is good service, and call the police. Tell them our location, and that you'll need a medic. I then need you to call my husband, and tell him what's going on. Can you handle that?"

June grabs Mrs. Brown's phone and does exactly what's told. Dr. Aldis makes her way down the hill using the mini flashlight on her keys.

"Hi, Mr. Brown! I'm so sorry. It's so late, but Mrs. Aldis told me to call you, because we are out here on dead man's bridge, and Terrell has been in an accident." She tried to get the message across with a clear voice, and without sobbing. Mr. Brown jumps up out the bed instantly grabbing his clothes, and keys.

"What accident? Who is this? How did you get my wife's phone young lady?"

"Well, Mr. Brown. This is June, your wife gave me her phone. Please come quick Terrell is in an accident on dead man's bridge." June hangs up, and Mr. Brown jumped up already getting dressed, and on his way.

"I'm almost there sweetie." Mr. Brown replies to the dial tone as he jumps in his F5, and speeds down the road.

Giving a quick text to the nanny that no one else was in the house, and she needed to keep and ear out for Ally.

By the time Mr. Brown pulls up, he is stopped by a road block full of medics, fire rescue, and a crowd of people. He noticed a young lady on her phone, pacing back, and forth behind the yellow caution blocks. He runs in her direction, in hopes that it's June. He didn't even acknowledge the two police officers that were chasing him down, telling him not to go in there.

"Sir! Where are you going? We're going to need you to step behind the yellow caution blocks, for your own safety." Says the officer with his hand on his right hip, and his finger pointed in the opposite direction.

"The fuck, you talking about. That's my son down there." Replies Mr. Brown, as June runs closer to the gate when she hears the phrase my son.

"Mr. Brown. He's down there."

"Where's Aldis?"

"She's down there with the paramedics." The officer gives the okay for him to come through, as they both run closer to the ditch to find his wife.

"I'm assuming you're June!"

"Yes, sir."

"Aldis, I'm here." Mr. Brown yells down into the ditch not knowing what his next move was supposed to be.

"We're wheeling him up right now." She yells back.

There were so many tubes, and wires Mr. Brown couldn't make out what exactly was going on.

That's my son, that's my boy done there. Was all Mr. Brown could think in that moment, as Terrell rolled across his very eyes on a stretcher. He knew he needed to be strong for Aldis, but deep down Darnell was already broken. Taken full responsibility for the dangers of the accident, he couldn't do anything but hold back his tears. Completely in his feelings, he reaches his hand out to Mrs. Brown to help her out of the ditch. Aldis was completely covered in dirt, grass, and her knees were soaked with muddy water.

"Thanks honey." She replied, as she released her hands from Mr. Brown. "Now, this is what's going on." Mrs. Brown takes a deep breath to remain in doctor mode, so she could explain everything clearly. Deep down, she wanted to fall apart, but knew it wouldn't help the situation.

"He has a couple broken ligaments, heart rate active, but he's unresponsive. Which, after all, is a good thing, because he would be in massive pain right now. But, I'm thinking he's in a coma."

"How bad of a coma?"

"I don't know, but I'll know something when we get him to the hospital, and run more test. All I can assume is that when he made his way, around the corner, at what seems to be a speed of 78 maybe 80 he hydroplaned trying to make the turn. That caused him to fly out the driver side window. I'm so glad the window was open, because if it was closed the damage could've been much worse, or even deadly. He didn't have his seat belt on, which I will deal with that later. From the outlook of the car, and where I found Terrell, once he flew out the window he hit that tree. He was out cold from there. The funny thing is that his car flipped over three times, and slide right beside him, and never touched him. It was literally one sixteenth of an inch from his body, and they both were upside down. Yes, I had them measure it, because it was a complete miracle. I guess that little prayer I prayed, worked."

"Excuse me, but Mrs. Brown, will you be riding with us?" The paramedics asked.

"No! Ma'am, I'll ride with my husband, but we are right on your trail."

"Yes, ma'am," the paramedic replied, getting into the ambulance.

The medics drive off with the Browns following, and June and her cousin trailing right behind them.

"I don't understand! Why didn't you ride with the paramedics?" Mr. Brown asked. Mrs. Brown didn't even reply, she just lifted her shirt and threw the glock 9 on the dash.

"Now you know."

10

The rest of the car ride was silent for the Browns. There was too much on both of their minds, which they weren't ready to discuss. Mr. Brown spoke with Aldis about someone picking up her car from the accident scene. That way, it wouldn't get stolen, or damaged. She agreed, as she gets dropped off at the back entrance, and hops out the car. While Mr. Brown found a parking spot in the front of the hospital with June, and they both rushed in.

"Hey, Mrs. Brown. There is no need for you to check in. Terrell's room is already set up, and he will be in room 109. Dr. Roberts is on call, and will be handling his file. I'm assuming you'll be the one that will be assisting him." Monica replied.

Monica was one of Aldis's head nurses in charge, and assisted her when she needed help. She had been at Dr.

Browns side since she took her CNA classes, and completed the field of nursing.

"You're absolutely right Monica. I'll check in early for my shift tomorrow, and work a double since I'm already at the hospital. My husband should be walking in the visitor's entrance, so please tell the receptionist to send him back.

"Yes, ma'am, I'll put it down on the charts, and it's back this way. Oh! What am I saying. You work here, you know your way around."

Monica heads back to the front area where there seems to be some commotion. Mrs. Brown headed to her office to change into her scrubs, and head off to Terrell's room, as Mr. Brown and June both trail into the main entrance to be greeted by the front receptionist.

"Are you Mr. Brown? If so, Terrell is all set up, and you can head back to room 109. Dr. Aldis is already back there, and I'm sure she's waiting for you. Monica filled me in on what was going on, so if you just enter those doors she's the back nurse, and will take it from there. By the way, I'm Dominique the head receptionist." Dominique shakes Mr. Brown hand, and looks directly at June without holding back.

"And you are?"

"I'm June! Terrell's girlfriend."

"Oh, I didn't know he had a girlfriend." Dominique started laughing, and placed her eyes back on Mr. Brown. He just grinned, and asked for direction to Terrell's room once more. June doesn't hesitate to follow before the receptionist quickly redirected her back into the lobby.

"Umm! I'm sorry miss thing, but you'll be waiting out here."

"What is it to you if I go back to be with my boyfriend? Miss Dominique."

"Like I said, the lobby is for friends, and the back is for family, so you'll be in the lobby."

June just walked away knowing that things could've gone in a completely different direction. She then takes a seat, and pulls out her phone to call her mother.

"Hey, Mom!"

"Hey, June! Why are you up this late? And, where is Tae?" Dawn replied. Completely panicked as to why her daughter was calling her this late at night.

June just took a deep breath. "Me and Tae are keeping tabs on Terrell. I got a phone call that he was in the hospital."

"Oh, yeah! I heard, he was in a very bad car accident."

"Yes, ma'am, he was."

"June, pleases just stay in the house. It's too dangerous for you to be out chasing a boy, and you know what happened last time. I don't need to call your uncle so I can know exactly where you are do I?"

"No! Mother. I understand. This is why I called you, so you wouldn't be worried when the word got out. Me, and Tae are right here watching movies."

"Ok June! Please prove me right, and behave."

"Yes, ma'am. I will, love you mother."

"Love you to June."

June hangs up the phone, to only think about the reason she was there in the first place. I can't believe I lied to my mother again, over this boy. I really must love him. Completely distracted by the phone call with her mother. She missed the action in the lobby with a couple of Terrell potential lady friends.

"What happen to him?"

"Is he ok?"

"I can't believe this happened to him." June walked closer to the front desk only to notice several of her high school friends in the lobby crying over Terrell.

This is the very reason I called my mother first. It don't take long for drama to spread around here. It most have gotten out fast about Terrell, because the streets were empty a hour ago. This is just plain crazy, how could it have gotten out that quick tho. I know this a small town, but really? These people are just plain nosey.

June reaches into her pocket, and pulls out another phone. I really can't believe I'm doing this, but some stuff I need to know. 5 missed calls from Stephanie, 15 from Mother, 7 from Candice, 2 From Joyce 3 from an Unknown number, and 3 from just really. Who the heck is Just Really?" June then takes the liberty to open the text. *"Hey Terrell I hope your okay, I heard you were in an accident. Hit me back."* Then it reads, *Terrell are you okay? I'm getting worried. Terrell let me know you're okay?* Who is this "Really" person, and they seemed really in tuned with Terrell. I have got to look up this number (325) 434-9876, as soon as I can. Like, really! Who is this person?

June still continued to scroll through his phone, asking herself question only Terrell could answer.

Junes name was called out several times, before she almost dropped Terrell's phone.

"What?" She screeched.

"Sorry to startle you, but I'm going to trust you with my phone.

"Oh, Hi Mr. Brown."

Mr. Brown just smiled. "No one should call, but the nanny, and if she does just let her know that we are still here, and won't be home until Monday morning. My phone will not pick up in the back, and I don't want to miss the nannies call."

"Yes, sir! I can do that."

"I'll be out periodically to check on you. By the way, good job at holding your own at the front desk. Sometimes it's best to walk away instead of running your mouth." Mr. Brown pats June on the shoulder then walks away.

"Wow! That was a close one, let me just put his phone away. "Beep" Terrell phone goes off again. *Terrell if you can read this, please text me back your room number.*

June just ignores the message, and then goes through all the messages between Stephanie, and Terrell. I see Terrell was right. It was more or less Stephanie, who was harassing him, but who is this Ally girl? Why does Stephanie want to see her? I hope it's not another one of his female friends.

June's mind is on overload, but she continues to read. *Terrell, I miss the bond we had, and I hope we can reunite our relationship so we can be a family.* Family? What is Stephanie talking about? *Terrell please let me see Ally! Man, I swear, you'll so petty.* A couple more message. *So, you and June together. I saw y'all riding last night. Terrell Ally's my daughter too.* Daughter! Terrell, and Stephanie have a daughter together. June's eyes, buck.

That's the little girl I always hear in the background. I thought it was his sister. Which, I never even thought to ask.

163

Why doesn't he talk about her? Him and Stephanie tho? He could've done way better. That's the one dude she slept with. *"The outcome was great, but nothing else was."* It all makes sense now. That's why she befriended me, to keep tabs on him.

This is just too much in one night. June thought to herself, as thing begins to play out in her head.

Okay, so let me see what's up with him, and Candice. *Hey cousin when you coming to see me?* This is nothing.

June looks up from her snoop Fest to the sound of a familiar voice. Here comes this trick, and why is she coming over here.

"Excuse me bitch, but don't think for a minute. I'm leaving you in this hospital with my man."

"Stephanie, Terrell is not your man. Please stop saying that." June replied softly. "He doesn't want anything to do with you."

Stephanie just sits beside June, as they both were just looking towards the front desk, where Dominique was sitting, waiting for something to pop off.

"I'm gon to talk to you like an adult. That's if you can understand that language. Terrell, and I have ties together. I will, and he will always be in my life, but that's something you'll never understand. See, when you have a bond with someone, like me and him it's something that can't be broken. I'll give you credit. You thought y'all were going to be together, but as you can see that dick belongs to me. So, I'm here now. You can just go home. Oh, and don't worry your mother called me. I covered for you! You're welcome."

June stayed poised thinking about what Mr. Brown said before replying back. She leaned in, with her elbows in her legs.

"Well! I thank you for what you feel is covering for me, but I just got off the phone with my mother, and she knows I'm staying with my cousin Tae. And, if it's any of your business she's right outside with her boyfriend, waiting for me if any BS should happen. Another thing, that bond you think you and Terrell have together, yeah, he told me. Her name is Ally. She's very beautiful, by the way. So, I can give you credit for that. See we! Meaning me, Terrell, and Ally. Have our park dates. Oh, you didn't know that, did you? Yeah, girl. We play on swings, feed the ducks, and walk the pond."

Almost laughing June starts feeling herself, because she knows now she's cutting deep. "How about y'all? Have y'all spent any time as a family? Have you been to any of her birthday parties? Do you even know how old she is? Oh! My stepdaughter will be three this year, and the birthday party we're planning is going to be amazing. Now I know this information surprised you, because I'm a little smitten myself! And trust, my dear. We don't want to have nothing to do with you. See why you thought you was coming for me, I just decide to go ahead, and meet you half way. Now, take that to the bank, and cash it in."

June eased back in her seat, and crossed her arms with complete joy. Stephanie couldn't believe the information just revealed to her. She couldn't help, but wonder where, and how did June of all people know all these things about Ally. Her eyes begin to water, but not one tear fell. She didn't want her to know that she had got the best of her. In the mist of all this, the eye contact was so deep that their souls met, and you could cut the tension with a knife. It took everything in Stephanie's power to refrain from punching her, but as soon as she balled up her fist Mr. Brown walks up to give June an update on Terrell.

"Hey! June." Darnell paused. "Shit, Stephanie! What the hell are you doing up here?"

"No worries, I'm leaving." Stephanie replied, without taking her eyes off of a smiling June.

"Well get the hell on" Mr. Brown watched Stephanie as she walked out the sliding doors. "She didn't bother you, did she?"

"No Sir! Sometimes it is just best that you just keep your mouth closed, and let them make a fool of themselves." Mr. Brown just laughed, and begins to update June on how Terrell was doing.

"I'm sorry for that June." Mr. Brown says, "but that girl is something evil. Well, Miss Lady since I like you, I'll feel you in on more details. Terrell has a couple of bruises, and some broken ligaments, but our main concern is that he is in a slight coma. I hope you're a firm believer in God, because we need all the prayers we can get at this moment."

"Yes, Sir! I am, but if you will allow me. Can I go back and see him."

"Sure! Here is my name tag, but only if you promise me you will get some rest, when you come back out, because I can tell you're not leaving."

"Yes, sir! I will."

Mr. Brown steps away, taking the time to update the nanny. *"I will not return until tomorrow morning."* Was all June heard before making her way down the hall.

"Miss Lady! You either sit down, or go in the lobby. But, all this walking back and forth must end" Dominique replies. June just waves her badge, and keeps walking.

This girl is getting on my nerves. If she just does her job as a receptionist, and stop worrying about me she may get some work done. June thought as she walked the short distance to Terrell's room. A very uncomfortable feeling overtook her body, as she grew closer to the door.

I really feel like I'm the cause of all this. She spoke out loud, as she stood at the door. The people walking pass gave her a look of you're crazy, and some gave a feeling of sadness, but she really didn't care at this point. She said a quick prayer, asking the Lord to fix as much of this as possible. Once finished, she knocked on the door, and was met by Aldis.

"Hey, Mrs. Brown. I didn't know you were back here."

"I have not left his bedside since we got here." Mrs. Brown didn't even take the liberty of looking up. She invited June in, and asked her to close the door behind her.

"Well, I can understand that. I would be the same way."

"So, I see you really like my son." Mrs. Aldis asked, as June sat in the seat across from her.

"Yes, ma'am. He's sweet."

"Yeah, and he fine too." June started laughing.

"Yes, ma'am."

"Yeah! I know June! I use to be a young lady too. So, I understand."

"Mrs. Brown, may I ask you something."

"Sure sweetie!"

"I was wondering, if I could have a minute alone with Terrell."

"Umm!! Sure honey, but just for a minute. Nothing longer than that. I guess I can get a cup of coffee. You know he's in a coma, and can't respond to anything you're saying."

"Yes, ma'am. I understand!"

Mrs. Aldis walks out the room, and heads to the nurses stand. June immediately grabs Terrell's hand, and gives it a tight squeeze.

"Terrell I am so sorry. I got you in this situation." Tears just begin to fall. "If I never got mad at you, and ran off, you wouldn't be here. I know you, and Stephanie had a pass, but I forgive you. I wish you could hear me. But, please wake up."

June kisses Terrell on the forehead, and adjusts his covers. Terrell if you can hear me I love...

"Okay! Miss Lady, I'm back." Mrs. Brown interrupts Junes one on one time.

"I'm sorry! Mrs. Brown. I just couldn't help it."

"No need to apologize sweetheart. I completely understand, because when you like someone you don't want to see them in a harmful position. You do just like him? Right?" June, completely in her feelings, disagreed.

"No, ma'am."

"No, ma'am! Please don't say it, June. Don't say you love him."

"Yes, ma'am! I love him. I can't help it, and I know it's only been a year since I've known him, but we just have that connection."

"Honey, you're only eighteen, you can't know what love is." June didn't even respond, because she wasn't sure herself what this feeling was. But, she knew it was a feeling she never felt before.

"Well, sweetie. I have to get Terrell comfortable, and it's pretty late in the night. I would feel bad to tell you to go home at this hour, so I'll see if we have an empty room. I still need you to speak with your mother, and let her know where you are, if you already haven't."

Mrs. Brown. I can sleep in the lobby, and yes ma'am I already spoke with my mother. I guess I'll update my cousin. Also, I kept an eye out on his vitals. They remained stable, according to his electrocardiograph."

"Wow, I'm impressed! How did you know the actual name for the virtual machine?

"This is my career goal. I want to be a nurse, or a doctor like you. So, In my spare time, I read medical books to educate myself on the medical field."

Mrs. Brown was completely floored. "Wow! Girl! Not only are you a virgin, but you got a good head on your shoulders. Yes, my dear! Love him, love him to death. You're exactly what he needs in his life. Just Know, this field is demanding, and will take a lot of hard work."

"Yes, ma'am! I understand. I'll be out in the lobby if you need me."

"Please send my husband in here?"

"Yes, ma'am!"

June walked out proudly, knowing she had Mrs. Brown's approval. "Dang! There is always commotion in this lobby."

June walked pass a female with blonde hair, and green streaks. Looking at her eyes you could tell she had dark green contacts, and red lipstick. This girl is very beautiful, but acting so ghetto. Still wondering what's going on, June gets side tracked by Dominique.

"Yeah, that's her" Dominique says.

"Nah, cuz that can't be her, she ain't even his type."

"I told you" Dominique replies. "She's real uptown saddidy."

"Umm, so I take it your little Miss June!"

"June, yes! Little not exactly. And you are?"

"That ain't yo business of who I am."

"Well, I'll take that as you think I'm Terrell's girlfriend, am I correct? Wait! Before you respond, let me just say, I am. You see, Terrell has no others, but me. Now if he flirted, or gave you the impression that he was single. Let me just apology from the both of us, because he is currently off the market." June just shakes her head, and allow her confidence to take full force. "Now! We thank you for your condolences, and concerns, but you're no longer needed."

"No this bitch didn't just go off on me like I'm some kind of job interview, or employment. Trick, I ain't worked, and ain't never had to. So, don't be calling yo bougie ass trying to fire me from Terrell." June just takes a deep breath, and shakes her head once more.

"Silly girl, or whatever you would like to be called. You know! Since it ain't none of my business. I will discuss this with you at a more appropriate time. I have some praying to do, and as you can tell. My boyfriend is in need of a more intensive care. Meaning, my hand to knee services. So! If you can understand that, I would like to excuse myself."

June just walks away still looking out the corner of her eye, to an over rowdy Tenkia. Dominique took the liberty of holding her cousin back, because she knew if a fight broke out, she would be held responsible.

"Dominique, this chicken head really thinks she's somebody. Girl, call me when this bitch leaves. Trust me! I'll be right outside. I would bust her head now, but I don't want you to get fired."

Tenkia walks through the lobby mean mugging June, letting her know by know means did she intimidate her. June, didn't move a muscle. She just kept walking with no regards to Miss ghetto's tactics.

June, sits two seats down from Mr. Brown where he appears to be sleeping. As soon as she gets comfortable he doesn't even open his eye's, or raise his head.

"You can't catch a break tonight can you miss lady? And from the looks of it, it's ongoing."

"I'm built for toughness, don't let this pretty face fool you. I wasn't raised in the ghetto, but I know much about the ghetto." Mr. Brown just balled up his fist for a fist pound, and told June she handled herself real well.

"Mrs. Brown would like to see you."

"I was just getting ready to head that way." Mr. Brown replied, as he got the visitor's card from June, and headed to the back. Things in the lobby begin to fade as time passed, but June stood strong for Terrell.

It's 4 A.M. In the morning, and I'm just now taking a nap. This is ridiculous. My cousin left me after her and blonde head got into it in the parking lot, and I've never seen so much drama in one night.

June pulled two hospital chairs together, and propped a step stool in the middle to make a bed. Terrell is full of surprises tonight, but that still don't take away from the fact that I still love him. Oh! My goodness! I love this boy. I love Terrell. June just sat with her head rested falling in and out of sleep. She finally got the peace and quiet she deserved.

Minutes passed, and June jumped up looking around from a very vivid dream. I'm still in the hospital. For a second she was perplex until she remembers why she was there.

Let me see if I can sneak back here, and see Terrell. It's 4:55 in the morning, the lobby's empty, and the receptionist is nowhere to be found. Let me do this fast before Dominique ugly self come back up front.

June eased back to room 109, but she is certain her eyes have deceived her yet again. I can't today, I just don't have the energy to deal with this BS. Why has he done this to me again? He just continues to pull me in his world, just to break me down. This can't be love. This just can't be.

June grabs her things, and runs out completely distraught.

11

What day is this? What's going on? Where am I? Why am I in so much pain? Terrell turns back and forth trying to remove plugs, and tubs. Completely confused about why he's in the hospital. He looks over to his left to focus on the person in front of him.

"Terrell, you're alive. You're okay. Don't worry, you're in the hospital, and stop removing those plugs."

"The hospital? I'm in the hospital, but why?"

"Shh, Terrell! Please be quiet, before someone hears you."

No! Why are you here?

"I just came to check on you, that's all."

"Why the hell are you checking on me? Where's my mom?"

"Because I care about you Terrell, that's all. I was told you were in a bad car accident. They said that both of your legs were broken. And, that you dislocated your shoulder. Another said, you had died, and they had to resuscitate you three times. I was so hurt, let alone, scared when I found out. So, I ran up here around 2:30 thinking no one would be here. I had panicked, because I needed to see for myself. To my surprise, there were so many people here. The lobby was completely full with our classmates, and nothing but drama. I finally got the chance to sneak in to see for myself if all the rumors were true, and I see that they were not."

"And, what the hell does this have to do with you?"

"I mean.. I care. However, you were in ICU with a broken leg, and some shoulder damage, but nothing major. The thing that I was most concerned about was you being in a coma."

"I was in a coma?"

"For two days, it's early Sunday morning almost 6 O'clock. So, yeah! Two full days, and when I tell you I was worried sick. I just didn't know what to do with myself."

Terrell just laid in the bed, staring up at the ceiling.

"Where is my mother? I need my mother! And, like I said before, what the fuck are you doing here?"

"It really doesn't matter, why I'm here. Just know I support you."

"Like hell it doesn't matter. Please just leave! I can't deal with this right now."

"Not until you reassure me your ok."

"I'm fine! So, go before I call the cops." Terrell place his hands on the call button.

"Just a little F.Y.I. Miss June was out here all weekend sleeping in the lobby. Which you told me, y'all were just friends! But, now is not the time for that. I'm just glad my boo is okay."

"Stop calling me your damn boo, and I'm pushing the nurses button right now!"

"Ok, I'm gone."

The nurse runs into the room in total astonishment.

"Terrell! You're awake."

"Yes, ma'am," Nurse Candice runs out into the hallway, yelling for Aldis.

"Terrell is up! He's out of his coma. Come quick, hurry. Okay, Terrell! Your mother is on her way. Let's just run some quick test. Do you know why you're here?"

"No, ma'am."

"Do you know what your full name is?"

"Yes, ma'am! Terrell Darnell Brown."

"How old are you?"

"I'll be 19 in a few weeks."

"Do you know who this lady is?"

"Yes! My mother." Aldis just broke down. She couldn't help but to drop to her knees at Terrell's bedside. I have to give all homage to God.

"Oh, Lord! My God! You are so good to me. My son is alive, and well. My baby! My sweet baby! Thank you Jesus! Lord, I thank you!" Mrs. Aldis then analyzes her son, as Candice just pats her on the shoulder.

"He's up Hun! He's alive and well!" She then walks out so they can have some private time.

"Son, how do you feel?"

"I'm ok! Mother can we go home? I really just want to go home!

"Terrell you're in a cast, and just woke up out of a coma. Your first question is to go home? I'm going to ask you again. Son! How do you feel?"

"I'm ok mom. I'm in a lot of pain, but nothing else.

"Do you know why you're here?"

"Yes, mother! A car accident, I do believe. I just want to go home. That's all."

"Okay, son. Let me see if I can pull some strings with the other doctors. I can't make you any promises, but maybe you can be released early under my care."

"Thank You! Mom" Aldis just looks at Terrell, wipes her tears, and begin to examine him again.

"Mother!"

"Terrell, I have to. I'm doing my job now. I'm not being your mother. I'm being your doctor, and there are a couple of things you must do in order for us to be aware your brain is functioning well with your body. You must go to the restroom on your own, which also meanings having a bowl movement. Walk around the hospital the best you can without passing out, or becoming fatigued. I would like for you to eat a solid meal, so I know you will be able to hold it down, and I'm signing you up for counseling. There will be know no questions around that. Even though your coma only lasted two days Terrell, there can be some serious emotional danger with that diagnosis, and I want you to be well prepared."

By now Aldis has walked around the bed, and removed all visible tubs from Terrell's body, and is still prepping him on the side effects that can come with being in a coma.

"Mom, I get it! Now can we go?"

"Can you stand now, or do you need my help?"

"No mother! I can stand. What the hell is this?"

"Oh! Sorry, Son. It's your catheter, and you watch your language."

"Sorry."

"You have two options. Either I can take it out, or I'll call Nurse Candice, and she can?"

"I'll take Candice."

"Boy, I gave birth to you."

"Exactly! That's why I'll take Candice." Mrs. Aldis just shakes her head, and calls Candice in the room to complete the job."

"I'm going to go get your release papers done. By the time I get all that worked up, and make my rounds you should be set to go."

"Candice, will you please keep an eye on Terrell, so I can get these things completed?"

"Yes, ma'am," Replies Candice, as Aldis walks out the room.

"Terrell, I'm going to need you to take a deep breath." Terrell complied, as Candice removed the catheter from his penis. She heard nothing, but grunts, and moans that followed.

"I'm sorry! I'm so sorry, but this is the only way. Are you okay?" Asked Nurse Candice, as she noticed Terrell is not quite the young man he use to be.

"At this point, I don't have a choice but to be."

"Okay! Well, I'm going to go ahead, and remove your bed sheets while you get dressed."

Candice laughs with a little shame as she walks out the room. Terrell finds the clothes that his father dropped off yesterday evening while on his way to work. He was in desperate need to take a shower, so he could get out of his hospital robe, but his cast wouldn't allow him to. Terrell reaches in his bag and yanks out the first pair of sweatpants he sees. His phone immediately drops to the floor, as he slowly reaches down, he feels a streak of pain run up the back of his spine. He held the phone in his hand for a little while as the pain left his body, and he did all he could to remember his passcode. The number 0608 popped in his head, and his phone clicked open. The first thing that came up was a note from June:

Dear Terrell,

Tomorrow is Sunday, and I really hate to have to leave you in this condition. Laying here in this lobby waiting for you to recover has sickened me, and I have grown to know that I have developed strong feelings for you. I don't want to scare you off by saying I love you, but deep down there is nothing else this could be. I've never felt this way about anybody, and I was overly excited about this new chapter, in what could've been our life. I even forgave the whole Stephanie situation, and was thinking of fun things for me, you, and Ally to do. Yes! I know all about your baby Ally, and from the look on your wallpaper, she's very beautiful. The thing that lead me to write this letter was that I didn't understand why Frank was in your room sobbing over your bedside? Now, I understand the concept bros before hoes, but him holding your hand, and kissing you on the forehead was what got me extremely baffled? I really almost lost all composure after the weekend I've had. I just can't bear to take on anymore drama. I mean there's no way around this one, because

everyone knows he's gay, but if there is any logical reason
please give me a call.

June

Btw: Yes, I went through your phone, and I've noticed you
put your birthday in several times as your password. I didn't
read any other messages, but the ones from you, and
Stephanie. I hope your phone gets back to you, because I left
it with the lady at the front desk after running out the rest
room from an upset stomach. I really hope you feel better.
Later!

"Are you ready?" Aldis was more excited than ever,
to have her son back. "Hello? Terrell!" Aldis yells one more
time out of fear. "Son! Oh, my goodness!" Aldis runs to his
side when she doesn't get a response out of him.

"Yes, Mother! I'm ready!"

"Boy! You scared the life out of me."

"Mom, I'm just trying to take all this in, everything's happening so fast, but I'm good." She takes a deep breath, so she can go over their plans for his discharge.

"Son, I understand there's a lot going on. This weekend has been one from hell, trust me I understand. But, from this moment on there will be no more secrets. I promise I will be upfront with you and discuss our problems. I don't want this to happen to our family again. Do you understand?"

"Of course mom."

Aldis pats Terrell on the leg as she sits beside him to go over her discharge papers. "I have to read over them with you, and of course you know we will follow protocol when we get home."

"I know. I just gotta get back into the swing of things. Who has Ally?"

"The nanny, and don't worry about that. Ally has been well taken care of. I'll be lying if I didn't say she hasn't been missing you, because she has. We didn't bring her up here to see you, because I didn't want to take the chance of scaring her, but she asked about you everyday. We told her that you were at basketball camp for the weekend. Your car on the other hand is completely totaled. I guess you can get that upgrade you been asking for. I'm sure that will make you happy"

"How am I going to stay strong for my baby?"

"Well, Son! You'll get there. Let's go! So, I can get you settled in at home. Your doctor released you under my care, and your father's down stairs waiting with the car."

"Mother, I've been through so much this weekend. I just can't deal with him right now."

"Terrell, at this point you don't have a choice. I can't leave my car here. Besides, I will be home with you for two weeks, maybe a month if I get my time approved. I will call the nurse to get your wheelchair ready, and we'll be on our way."

"I don't need a wheelchair."

"Terrell! You will be in that wheelchair. I already got your stuff together. Is there anything else you want to talk about."

"No, ma'am."

Terrell just sat at the end of the bed, waiting. Finally, his four wheel ride arrived, as he was quietly wrapping his mind around the fact that Frank was at his bedside when he woke up. Then there was the letter from June that didn't make things better. Nevertheless, He was very thankful that the doctor released him, and although he only met two out of the three requirements to leave. Aldis agreed to fix him some homemade chicken soup, as soon as he got home. He would still be on bed rest there, but at least home is where he wanted to be.

The first thing he requested was to take a hot bath. A pain pill was calling his name, and seeing Ally was the most important. But, he needed to deal with this car ride, which he knew was going to be mentally brutal.

Mr. Brown pulls the car around, and Aldis rolls Terrell out the front door, handling the wheelchair with ease.

"Let me help you with that honey."

"No! I'll do it myself." Terrell tries to enforce his feeling, but they were overlooked.

"No you will not!" Mrs. Aldis replies. "Now, I don't care if you two don't speak to each other, but you're going to ride together." Terrell just sits back, and puts on his seatbelt, without speaking a word. Darnell closed the door, and walks around to the other side to meet his wife with her keys.

"I'm sorry honey, but Processive brought your car here instead of the house."

"It's okay, babe. I told them too, so the both of you can hash things out with words this time, instead of blows."

"Well, what should I say?"

Aldis made a few hand gestures, soon unspoken words, and Mr. Brown knew he must clear the air with his son, before he returned home. Darnell just held his head down looking for ways to strike a conversation when he got in the car.

"Son, have you heard from your pretty little girlfriend, June." Terrell doesn't respond, waiting for this to be over. "Yeah! Son, she's a good one. I would do all I can, to hold on to that one." Terrell doesn't budge he's only thinking, yeah, don't screw her like you did the last one. "Look, Son! You can sit over there, and be quiet. But, I'm going to tell you what truly happened, so we can put this behind us."

"Man to man, I really don't want to hear it" Terrell finally opens up.

"Truthfully, I put all blame on me."

"Dad, really I don't have time for this. No, matter what, at the end of the day. Ally's not mine, she's yours."

"That is absolutely right son, but just please hear me out."

12

"Ally is mine. Your mother and I were absolutely wrong for allowing things to go the way that they did. At the time we were having a lot of marital problems. That's something you may, or may not understand. But, for the most part, you were in basketball practices, training camps, and focused on other things to even notice all the fussing, and fighting we did. We always tried to refrain from doing any of those things around you.

Nevertheless, at the time when we had our biggest problems! I was a bar whore. Every weekend, if I wasn't at your games, or working late, I was at the bar. This is where I met Stephanie. I don't know what Stephanie told you, but rape was something that definitely didn't take place. I can't remember the bar's name, but it was over there on third and tenth. It's a twenty one and older crowd. All I can assume is that she used a fake ID to get in."

"Dad, I really don't want to hear no more" Terrell replied, knowing exactly how it will end.

"Well, you're going to listen. This situation has caused major damage to my family, and as a man, it's my responsibility to fix it. Anyway, we both were tossing back shots at the bar, and she asked, Why was I alone? I told here a long day's work, and the conversation continued. Now you know how bold and forward Stephanie is. So, I was getting ready to leave before things got too heavy. She then offered to buy me a drink. And, of course, I stayed, because it's very uncommon for a female to offer to buy a round. This is what drew my interest as to who this lady was. We had a couple more shots, and the conversation deepened. I spoke to her about our marital problems, and she explained that she was going through the same thing, but the only difference was that she wasn't married. I mean she laid it on thick.

This young lady can be very seductive when she wants to be. Her field of study should be in marketing, because she can draw you in with the intent to get what she wants. Moving on, more drinks lead to use on the dance floor where things really got heated. I then explained to her that, I had to go, because I was going into the office the next morning. She was very understanding at this point, and we walked each other out.

We exchanged numbers in hopes that we could do it again. When she asked if I could drive her to her car. Of course, I obliged, and welcomed her into my vehicle. I went to her side of the door to help her in the car, and she instantly unzips my pants, and performed oral sex on me. I couldn't resist, because at this point I was buzzed myself, and the feeling of a woman's desire was much needed."

"Dad, that's enough." Terrell tried to stop his dad, although he wanted to hear more.

"Son, just let me finish. Where was I? So, people started coming out the bar. I quickly grab her by the shoulders, and told her lets get in the car first. We jumped in, and she tries to straddle me. I let her know there's a hotel right up the road, and we can go there. I asked her if she was sure she wanted to get a room, she agreed, and then finished what she started in the parking lot."

As the story prevailed, and the tension softened, Terrell began to ask questions.

"Dad, I don't understand how you could do that to mom? I would never do that to the woman I love." Terrell just shook his head, not understanding that those few simple words were signs of forgiveness.

"Son, when you're married, and you get lack of attention at home, any attention seems like good attention. Even when it's not! I hope you remember that when you get married, so you won't take the road I've followed.

Anyways, by now we're at the hotel. This girl is damn near naked in the lobby. I'm literally holding her tittes in my hands so her nipples want show. I got the closest room to the ground floor, and started putting in that work.

The next morning I rolled over, and she was gone. I rushed, and put my clothes on for my walk of shame. And, by the time I got to the car, my phone beeped. I just knew it was you mother about to give me the business, but when I looked down it was Stephanie. The text reads: *"I really enjoyed you last night, you were amazing."* I replied: *"How did you get my number?"* Forgetting I gave it to her before the sexual encounter took place. She simply said: *"You are one of the largest real estate agents this side of Texas, Right?"* I just shot back with a *"lol"* and never heard from her again.

After a month, or two, your mother, and I decided to reconcile our differences. I told her about my one night stand, and she told me about her dirt. We both asked for forgiveness, and brushed it under the rug. Later within that month, I get a text from an unknown number. They wanted to meet about some property they were interested in. Of course I agreed, and asked for the information. They sent me some bogus address that wasn't listed, and we met some where close by.

When I pulled up to the location she asked if I remembered her, and of course, I didn't. She had no makeup on, and her hair was pulled up in this mess of a bun, she also appeared very scared. I then asked her where were her parents located, because at this point I knew it wasn't about real estate. Once she gave me the rundown of what happen, and who she really was. I called my attorney, and your mother. They then handled the case from there."

Terrell just sat quiet absorbing the information carefully making sure he didn't miss anything.

"I still don't understand how, I got involved?" Terrell asked, still confused on his part in this situation.

"By the time we met with Stephanie, and her parents. They had already put her out of their home, and into the apartment she's in now. They were so embarrassed that their sixteen year daughter was pregnant, and let alone it was with a black guy. Her parents felt that was their only way out. So, when Ally was born everyone just assumed that she was you, and Stephanie's baby. By then, y'all had developed a close friendship. Which, in our legal documents it states that we can't discuss any of this information with outsiders, or legal action will take place. So, when people would say "Terrell and Stephanie baby is so cute." We never corrected them. That's how you became the outside father.

"Y'all still could've told me!

"Yeah, you're right. But, the timing was perfect, so we just let it be. Basically, Son! Even at my age, I'm learning to deal with things just like you are. We're learning to forgive, and let God have his way. Still at the end of the day, the truth is always the best way, and always communicate. A lot of this could've been avoided had me, and your mother talked things out. We both clearly let our emotions get the best of us, and it only deepened the problem." Darnell begins to pull the car to the side of the road. Terrell became more confused about what was going on, but didn't ask any questions.

"With that beginning said, Terrell do you have any question for me."

"No dad! Why?" Terrell just sat back, and looked out the window.

Darnell unbuckles his seat beat, put the car in park, and looked Terrell straight in his eyes.

"Well, I have one for you! What were your plans for this?"

Darnell reached into his glove compartment, and nicely placed the glock 9 on the dash. Terrell completely forgot about the gun he had before the accident took place. The look of disappointment took over both guys, and Terrell could only think if things went in a different direction, how would things have ended.

"Dad, I wasn't thinking!" Terrell said with tears in his eyes. "I was just so mad! I mean you think about it. Your daughter is not your baby, and the actual father is your father. Then, not only is it true, but is was told by Stephanie. You would've been pissed off too, and would've done the same thing."

"Yeah! You right, but as you can see, acting off your emotion doesn't get you know where. What was that gun going to do? Terrell if you would've killed me, thank God you didn't. Ally wouldn't have neither one of us. You would be in jail, and I'm 6 feet under. What if you missed your shot, and hit your mother. Better yet, Ally? How would you have lived that down? This is why I'm telling you. Even if you're mad, you have to think about the things you're doing, because there is always a conclusion to every situation. You decide whether it ends on a good note, or on a bad one. It's your decision.

"Dad, I wasn't thinking like that at that time."

"Son, neither was I. That's why you never handle things with a firearm. The fight was bad enough. I'm still hurting from that, but we're both still here to tell the tale. This is why I'm telling you Terrell, to think about things, before you act on it."

Darnell took the gun, and put it back in the glove box. Terrell didn't even reply from trying to hold back more tears, and Darnell was starting to break down himself. Knowing how badly this could've ended. Darnell, then eased back onto the road, and headed home in complete silence.

"Dad!" Terrell wanted to apologize to say the least, even though he was still mad about the situation.

"No! Terrell! Not right now. Let's just soak this in, and give homage to God. I'm just happy I still have a life."

Terrell just looks out the window in agreement. As, Darnell's timing was completely perfect, because Terrell could still see pieces of residue from his accident as they cross over dead man's bridge.

13

The car ride was still silent, and yet so cold. Terrell and Darnell both had no more words for each other, besides the acknowledgment of what was shared. Terrell couldn't do anything but wipe his tears. Still hurt from knowing that Ally wasn't his daughter. Darnell knew that this had put a burden on the relationship that he had developed with his son, but wished by the grace of God Terrell would find some way to forgive him. Both their hearts were heavy, and they couldn't even look each other in the eye, as they pulled up to the house.

"Who is that lady?" Terrell asked, as he stared out the car window.

"I don't know, but I will find out."

Darnell gets out the car to size up the situation. This brown tone lady, weighting in at no more than 160 pounds, was everything a man could ask for. Hips from a god, and a butt that could make any man kneel, and ask for her hand in marriage. Then she had the nerve to wear a sun dress. In his favor the wind was blowing just right, where you could see every dent of her curves. The lady was just bad! She stood at 5'6, and had golden brown hair, with just a touch of blonde streaks.

Terrell couldn't keep his eyes off her. Her natural beauty seems to look familiar, but he couldn't quite place her. Darnell just smiled at her beauty, as he walked passed to lend a hand to his son. He first needed to make his acquaintance.

"Hi, I'm Darnell Brown, but most know me as DD." She obliges back, and asks if she can be of any help.

"No! Ma'am, I can handle this one, but thanks anyway."

"Dang, she fine!" Darnell thought. But, of course it slips out his mouth, as he helps Terrell get out of the car. Terrell looked at his father, and smile in agreement. Using his crutches, Terrell makes his way to the door, as this female goddess follows.

"Hi there, you must be Terrell?" Terrell Just reaches out his hand in courtesy, and once she smiles he then knew exactly who she was.

"Why don't we all make our way into the house," says Aldis, as they all walk in with the pleasure of allowing Dawn to walk in first.

"Wow! What a beautiful home Aldis."

"Thank You!" Mrs. Brown replied, with a smile on her face. She then offers a seat to Mrs. Avery, and a bottle of water.

"Oh! I'm fine, I won't be long. I know you're getting Terrell adjusted to being home, and after such a terrible accident."

"Yeah, things will be a little shaky around here, but I'm sure we'll manage. I'm just glad my baby is okay."

"So, what can we do you for, Mrs. Avery?" Mr. Brown cuts in with his own concerns about the visit.

Dawn just slowly turned her head in the direction of Terrell. While thinking about the proper way to ask him about his relationship with June, without coming off as being disrespectful.

"I actually was asking your mother Terrell. If she knew anything about where June could possibly be located. She has gone missing, and I haven't been able to make contact with her. So, I was hoping that maybe, she made contact with you?"

"Um, ma'am, I..."

Terrell couldn't even express what was going through his head. He could only recap the letter she had written in his phone. He then became fidgety, and nervous, and looked at his father for help.

"Take your time sweetie," Dawn replies. "I don't want you to think over things. I'm just a little concern, and I knew the last time I spoke with her, she was telling me about you. I already knew she stayed the night with Tae, and that they were going to meet up with her friend Stephanie this morning to come see you in the hospital. Then out of know where I get a call from Stephanie this morning, and she told me the last place she seen June was at the hospital last night. She then gave me your address and phone number, and said if you're not at the hospital you would be home. So, instead of calling I took the liberty of stopping by to formally introduce myself."

Terrell's eyes grow big, and with no words he slowly made his way out the kitchen, and placed himself on their very expensive Bobkona Suede gray limited edition sofa. Mrs. Avery propped his feet up, and served him water, and his pain medication. Mr. Brown had no words, just hearing the name Stephanie made him tense up. But, he was curious to hear exactly how much she knows about the situation. And, If June and Stephanie are friends, how much does June know? Because, the exchange of words at the hospital between the two, one couldn't tell that they were associated.

Before things could go any deeper Mrs. Brown stepped in to change the dynamics of the conversation.

"Well, I'm certain Mrs. Avery that Terrell hasn't seen her. However, she did stop by the hospital early this morning, but Terrell wasn't awake from his coma just yet. So, I'm not sure what to tell you. "

"I'm so sorry." Mrs. Avery said, startled with embarrassment. "I see, now is not the time to be asking Terrell any questions, but as a mother we just get worried about our children. I'm sure you understand Mrs. Brown. Sometimes I let my emotions get the best of me, and maybe over think the situation."

"Trust me, I completely understand." replies Mrs. Brown. Terrell just remained quiet, and Mr. Brown offered to show Dawn to the door.

"Well, like I said, you have a very beautiful home, and again I'm sorry. Here is my number if you guys should see June." Mrs. Avery hands Aldis her number as she rubs her hand across the top of the couch. She gave her blessings to Terrell, and begin to walk towards the door.

"Thank you so much dear, and it's been a pleasure." Mrs. Brown followed Dawn to the door to be sure she left properly. "And, if I hear from June, you will be the first person I call."

Mrs. Avery walks out the door, and passes the big hole in the garage, before thinking Aldis again.

"Just keep walking." Dawn mimics under her breath, as she can tell there's more to this household than what's being told.

14

Dawn gets in her 2015 C Class Mercedes Benz, and hits the streets. She hopes to hear from June before nightfall, so she won't have to get the law involved.

Those people are weird, she thought to herself. They have such a nice home, but there was a big, I mean a big hole in the garage door. It looked like someone took a bomb, and just blow it up, and those fools were walking around like it wasn't even there. I really wanted to know what happened, because if this is the family my child will be around, they go have to do better than that. Anyway, let me call Clay, and tell him what just happened.

After having her own mental conversation Dawn called Clay to see if he's heard from June.

"Hey, Clay!"

"Hi honey, how are you?" Mr. Avery was happy to hear from his wife, which he hadn't all morning.

"Have you seen June?"

"I'm great; my day is going very well, thanks for asking!"

"I'm sorry! How is your day going? Say's Mrs. Avery with the least of her worries.

"It's going Dawn, but as far as June, I can't say that I have."

"Well, please call her! I can't make contact with her, and maybe she'll answer for you."

"Hun, please relax. You're over thinking things, she's fine! Trust me! She will show up."

"Will you promise me that you'll call her?"

"Yes, Dawn! I have to go now. I have a client."

Mr. Avery then hangs up the phone, and pulls out his cell phone with a quick text, *call your mother*. My work here is done. I'm sorry, sir! But, you know how it is to have a concern wife when it comes to children." Clay just smiles, and shakes his head.

"Now, sir! How may I help you?"

"Hi! Clarence Avery. I'm John Lace, I'm with child protective services, and I've been recommended to do an open case for you. Now the matter that has been reported is very serious, and is not to be taken lightly." Clay just busted out laughing.

"Child protective services. Oh, ok! Really? Now, who sent in that ridiculous complaint? And, when did y'all start coming out to peoples jobs for questions"

"Well, sir, that's something that I really can't share with you, but I just wanted to come and talk to you personally. I didn't want any other accusations to take place."

"Like what accusations?" Clay replied, as he couldn't stop laughing. He could only think this little ungrateful brat has called social services.

"Look Sir! There is nothing I can do, or tell you. I have never, nor will I ever touch a minor, and who ever called you is sick in their damn head."

"Well, Clarence! Never once did I say you touched a minor, so that's a red flag within its self. I was just coming to introduce myself as your case handler, before things got to another level. So, this minor that you didn't touch, does she or he have a name."

"It's Mr. Avery to you, not Clarence."

"Excuse me, Mr. Avery. I'm just doing my job, and it requires a visit to the offender. Take that how you please, but in this book its called step one." Mr. Avery just looked at John with no response.

"John Lace!" Mimicking John's last name once more "Lace," Clay asked. "Do I know you?"

"No, sir! I don't believe we've met before."

"Are you sure?" Mr. Avery replies. "You seem very familiar, like I've seen you before."

"Well, I do apologize, but no. Now! This minor, does he or she have a name?"

"I don't have anything to say on that issue. It's complete bullshit. Now that I'm done speaking on that. You may want to follow me home, because I'm telling you now, when I get a hold to that daughter of mine." Clay just shook his head. "We will need more than a case worker, and that's for sure."

John Lace just looked very concerned, and jotted down some notes. He looked up at the big reflector mirror in front of him, and noticed Clarence staring at him.

"I still can't believe you had the nerve to come up in here, and insult my intelligence."

"Well, sir! I just wanted to touch base with you, but I'm going to leave before this goes into a different direction."

John gets up from his authentic leather black chair, and heads for the door. He then extended his hand as a good bye jester, but Mr. Avery just holds the door open.

"Dude, please! You just insulted my character, and you think I'ma shake yo hand. Man, bye! Leave my office before a real case worker is needed for yo ass."

"I'm sorry, but is that a threat?" They both stood face to face adjusting their collars, before either reacted.

"No! John Lace, that's a promise." Lace just grinned as Mr. Brown slams the door, and calls Mrs. Avery.

"Hey, babe! No contact with June has been made, but I'm headed out the door as we speak. We have got to talk, as soon as I get home. I've had a day from hell, and it's because of that brat of a daughter."

"Clay, I thought we was going out to dinner?"

"We are dear, I'll be there shortly give me thirty minutes."

Mr. Avery just hangs up the phone, and starts straightening things on his desk.

"So, did you get anything John?"

"Yeah! That you have a jerk as a husband."

"Don't talk bad about Clay, he's a good man. He just been acting weird lately with June, and I need to know why."

"Dawn, are you sure he's a good man? He seems cocky and a little too sure of himself! I will be more than happy to bring him down a foot, or two."

"John, he was good enough to take care of our family when you didn't."

"I know, but Dawn at that time I wasn't ready to be a father. Well, let me say. I didn't know what true fatherhood was. So, I missed out on a lot of things in June's life.

"Yes, you did John. But, I will always, give credit, where credit is due. You didn't miss not one birthday party, or school event. Clay or June didn't know who you were. I was the only one that knew what was up, but I just wish you were there personally, not as a bystander. For the sake of June, you know. I mean, she just found out Clay wasn't her real father, and I know she took that hard. She just didn't want to admit to it."

Lace grabs Dawn hand to show compassion. "I completely understand, dear. But, I'm more than ready now than ever. I thought I had another chance with the little one we lost last year, but in due time, we will be a family." John kisses Dawn on the cheek. "Will I see you later?"

Mrs. Avery just smiles, and replies in a flirty way, "Maybe." She then pulls off, and text June once more, as she watched John Lace walk across the parking deck with a smile on his face.

Minutes later, Clay finally jumps out of his seat after catching up on a little paper work. Thinking! Man, when I see June, that's her ass. Clay grabs his phone to see a missed text from June. *"Ok loser!"* Clay just shakes his head, and speaks out loud. This damn child ain't got no respect, but that will be fixed here shortly.

Clay looks in the mirror as he walks into the elevator doors. He calls his self checking me. I'm a well established man. What I look like thirsting over a minor! Case closed.

By the time clay got to his car, he became more frustrated, and the condition of his car didn't make it any better.

Who in their right mind would flatten my tires? Clay asked himself, as he pulled out the knife that was sticking out the driver side tire. Clay makes his way around the whole car to check for any more damage, and long behold the back tire is out too. Well, I'll be damned. Let me call Alfa, and my wife.

"Hey, honey! You will not believe this, but someone has slashed both my tires. I won't be home in enough time for dinner. So, please call me when you get this voicemail."

Still in complete shock. He stood by the hood of his car, patiently waiting on Alfa. I bet it was that punk John

Lace. Clay said loudly, as he slammed his Alexander Amosu black blazer to the ground.

"Yes, sir, it sure was me! You got a problem now?" John Lace said as he walked slowly around the concert pole where he had been waiting for Clarence. He was very offended by the conversation that they had earlier, and was taking matters into his own hands.

"Hell! Yeah, I got a problem." Clay, says as he turns around to confront Lace who was standing at the tail end of the car.

"Dude! I got a problem with you too," Lace replied, stepping differently in Clay face. "You're in the way of my family."

"Family? Fuck yo family. Do you see my car dude? Tires ain't cheap, especially not on a Benz."

Lace grabs Clay around the neck, choking the pure life out of him. It happened so fast, that Clay didn't have a change to react, or defend himself. All he could do was listen to Lace speak into his right ear.

"I can give a damn about your car. I'm telling you now. You lay one good finger on my daughter, and you will have to deal with me."

Lace released Clay, looking to square up, but Clay still was trying to get an understanding of what the hell was going on.

"First off, get your hands off me." Clay pushes Lace away with force, as he staggers from trying to catch his own breath, and not fall to the ground. "Who exactly is your daughter, and what does that have to do with me?"

"Who is my daughter?" Lace rushed back into Clay's face "June, that's who!"

"What the hell? Excuse me, but did you say June?" Clay said, more confused than before. Wait! Partner! June is my daughter. She doesn't have any other man in her life, but me. Except for that one bastard, who left a pregnant woman out in the cold, and forced her to take care of herself. Now, I do know him, and now you expect to come back into their life, like nothing happened. Man, get the fuck out of here. Where the fuck were you when I was paying for doctors visits, buying diapers, school trips, birthday parties, driving lesson, and now college. Man, please! You will never be her father, or live up to what I have done for her. When she becomes a doctor, she'll take the time to thank me, because you ain't done shit."

"Oh, trust! I've been here, the whole damn time, fuck boy. I haven't missed one birthday party, or school recital. I still got pictures from my baby girl's first graduation, and I will have some from her last. Don't think, because you didn't know me. I wasn't there, because I've been here. Since the sun came up, on the day she was born, and will be, when the sun goes down on the day I die."

"Hold on, hold up! I knew, I saw yo ass before. You are that weird guy that's always in the shadows lurking. I remember a couple times when I made Dawn aware that you were there. She said, *To just ignore you, and that you were probably just a friend of a friend.*

"I don't care what she said to you. I'll continue to lurk, until I get my chance to meet my daughter. So, until then, nothing better not happen to my baby girl. Unless you want me back. Not only to beat yo ass, but that will probably be your last day living. And, please be more careful, because you almost raise another one of our babies."

Lace took a step back, and walked backwards towards the exit until he felt comfortable to turn around and walk away.

Clay just stood at a loss for words. What the fuck? He yelled, but could only hear his echo, and a car burns rubber.

How dare she? How could Dawn do this to me? We're married. She's supposed to be my rib, my backbone, and she does this."

Clay picks up his blazer, brushed it off, and was still lost in his thoughts. He was thinking of everything that happened over the years. He started to understand, that wasn't his baby she lost.

That's why she didn't want to go to counseling with me. That's why she's been missing in action, not given a damn if we're intimate, or not. This bitch has been lying, and having an affair the whole damn time. June became her only concern, and I was always last on her list.

"Sir! Is this the vehicle?" the Alfa agent asked, as he interrupted Clay. He was so startled he was ready to throw blows until he realized who was talking.

"Oh! Yeah, take it. As a matter of fact call another agent, I need a rental."

"Yes, sir! I definitely can do that." Clay then pulls out his phone to call Dawn.

"Hello,"

"Damn, you answered on the first ring! Hey! Did you make contact with June?"

"Oh, yeah babe. I'm sorry, I should've called you. She said, "Her phone had died, and she lifted it in the car to charge. So, by the time her, and her friend Maya came back from lunch. She was going to call me, but I called her first. She'll be headed home afterwhile tho. We still have to talk to her, because she lied about not going to see Terrell"

"Well, if you heard my voice mail, I'm still stock here waiting on Afla, but I'll be home right after."

"Okay, babe. But, there's no need to rush. I've ate, and Junes headed home."

"Okay, he's working on my car now. I'll just go back to my office, so you don't have to wait up."

"Love you sweetheart."

"You too!"

Clay hangs up the phone, jumps in his rental, and heads off. This has really pissed me off. He pulls two houses down from his own. Tears begin to flow, and he wiped them as soon as he felt one drop.

Hell No! Fuck that crying bullshit, this bitch got me fucked up. I ain't about to lose no sleep over this. Now, I just got off the phone with her ass. Where is she going? I should run her monkey ass over.

Dawn pulls off as Clay trails. I knew it. I knew something was up with her. Clay trails until they both pull into their favorite restaurant. 1424 Bistro!

What the heck is she doing here? He says, while waiting until she gets out, but she doesn't. Dawn just sits for over ten minutes. Clay's phone, then beeps and the text read:

Hey babe, just checking on you. XOXO   **8:30P.M**
I'm still here, maybe all night, but I'll call you when I leave the
office.   **8:32P.M**
K!!!!!!   **8:33P.M**

Dawn then hops out her car, and heads into the entrance, only to be embraced by John Lace.

She's such a liar. She's a damn fraud. Clay looks out his car window, and witnesses his cheating wife with the man he just had an altercation with.

I will never break our vows. Got me all up in the church, and talking about what God has brought together, let know man tear apart. Long behold she running these streets like a hoe. No worries! I'ma fix this shit, right now.

Clay jumps out his car and storms into the restaurant. By this time Dawn is seated, and John Lace goes into the man's restroom. Clay waits at the entrance to think of the best direction to go with this situation.

Now, I can be loud and unpleasing, or I can beat her at her own game.

Clay grabs a menu, and heads for the door. Jumps back in his car, and heads home. I got something for this loose bitch. She will learn today.

Clay walks into the house, place the menu on the front entrance table, takes a shower, and goes to bed. Two hours later Dawn returns home, and throws her key directly next to the menu.

What in the heck is this? Dawn thought to herself. Dawn runs up stairs, straight to June's room to find her sleep.

"Hey boo! What's up?"

"Nothing mom, I'm sleeping. I've had a very long weekend, and I'm tired."

"Oh, yeah! Tell me about it!" June just throws the covers over her head.

"Mom, please! I will in the morning. Just please let me rest."

"Ok, honey! Why did you bring a menu home from 1424? Is that where you and Maya ate?"

"I didn't." June replied, and passed back out.

Dawn just stood for a minute. Completely baffled about the menu. She forgot to mention that she knew about her meeting with Terrell, but Dawn needed to think quick on her feet.

It's no big deal. I can always say I was meeting with the parents of a new client. Dawn's thoughts still were running ten miles an hour when she entered her bedroom. But, was still wondering how the menu got home. She just left 1424 Bistro, and didn't see Clay, or June walks in. Considering she sat close enough to the door to watch everyone who entered.

"Hey!" Clay replied. When he heard the door opened.

"Clay, I thought you was working late?"

"I was, but decide to cut it short. I tried to wait up for you, but I must have fallen back out. Honey, are you okay? You look a little pale, and scared."

"Oh, no! I'm fine. I just thought something was wrong when I pulled up to an unknown car. So, I ran in to check on June, that's all."

"Yeah, that's the rental they gave me until my car is fixed, which will be first thing in the morning."

Dawn didn't say another word, she wasn't about to offer any information that wasn't asked.

"Come to bed," Clay replies. "I've missed you."

"Let me get comfortable first, and I'll be right there."

Dawn sprints to the bathroom to take a bird bath, and then climes into bed. Knowing exactly the night she just had with Lace, which was nothing short of amazing, but she couldn't let that show.

"My dear, you smell so good."

Nerves as ever Dawn asked, "What are you doing?"

"Foreplay, Boo!" Clay replied, as he went under the sheets.

Throughout his pain, Clay still managed to make love to his wife until she fell asleep.

The next morning Dawn woke up to an empty bed, and a brown box full of her things with a label that read:

These things belong to John Lace. Dawn then opened the note that was attached.

Dawn last night was incredible. You put in that work like I never thought you could, it's just too bad it was our last encounter. You see, I know all about you, and John Lace. I saw yo bitch ass, meet John at OUR favorite restaurant. That was so disrespectful. I would never do anything like that to you. I would've spoken to you in person, but it really looked like you two was enjoying your night, and I didn't want to take the measures of going to jail. Just for slapping a low down bitch like you. Oh, I'm sorry! I've found Jesus, so please disregard that last statement. How about this, I've packed your belongings, so be out by the time I get home, and we won't have a problem.

Thanks, Clay daddy!

Dawn just sat at the edge of the bed. You know what, who cares. I'm not going nowhere. He talks a good game, but ain't go do nothing. What man leaves a note for a woman to leave their house? His bitch ass couldn't even tell me to my face. Then he had the nerve to have sex with me. Yeah, we'll see.

Dawn then yells across the hall for June to get ready for school. Throws the note back on the box, makes her bed, and dashes into June's room.

"It's your last full day pumpkin. How do you feel? My little valedictorian."

"Mom! Please! I'm fine, and graduation ain't until Saturday.

"Yeah, I know. But, that's only a week away. Any plans?"

"No! Mother. I'll be here with you until my first day of college."

"What colleges have you chosen?"

"Mother, listen. I'm heading to school, and we can talk about it, when I get out. As a matter of fact! I'll take you out to dinner when I get home.

"Sounds good to me," replies Dawn. "Here are your keys Hun. Please be careful, and I give you permission to check on Terrell on your way home. That's if his parents are there. I'm trying to give you a little room to grow without me, because I won't be here forever. But, I've already met his parents, and they seem like pretty nice people. Keep in mind, I said seem, and I know Saturday you went to the hospital to see him, don't think I didn't know. I'ma let that one slide since Tae was with you."

"Yes, ma'am!" June replied in shock, trying to come to terms with the fact that her mother was being so lenient all of a sudden.

June knew it wasn't in her plans to go see Terrell. She needed to get more information from Frank, as to why he was in Terrell's room. He was doing all the things that she should've been doing, but she definitely wasn't about to tell her mother since she finally got the okay to go to Terrells house.

15

June grabs her keys after kissing her mother, and speeds off to school. When she pulls up, she does her normal routine of checking herself in the mirror, and applying lip gloss. The school seemed dead as she entered, but she was glad this was the last full day.

"Hey, June!"

"Hi! Maya. Where is everyone? The school looks empty."

"It's senior ditch day."

"Well! Dang, no one told me."

"Yeah, I didn't get the text either."

"I got to catch up with Frank, have you seen him?"

"All the seniors went to Polo's for ditch day. So, I'm sure Frank is with them even though he won't graduate until next year. What's going on with you and Frank?"

"Nothing really, I'm about to ride out to go meet him. You can come with me if you want to."

"Girl No!" Maya replies. "Every time I go to Polo's somebody starts fighting, or the cops are called. The last time, mace was sprayed. I'll pass, but you be safe."

June leaves the school headed to Polo's. She was thinking, Maybe I should stop by Terrell's first, and just speak. Then, the thought of getting the information from Frank became more important. That way she would know where the conversation should go when she does make time to talk to Terrell.

Maya didn't lie. Polo's is off the chain. The early morning crowd was full of teenagers, and it looks like the whole school is in here.

Let me park on the street, that way I'll be able to get out. Just in case something jumps off.

June steps out of her car, and the first person she sees is Stephanie. June just rolled her eyes, and mumbled this chick. "I should call her out her name, but that's still too respectful."

June just keeps walking as Stephanie acts as if she didn't even see her. Entering the building June wasn't really ready for the atmosphere. Polo's was already an after school teen club, where the young could go, and hang out with their peers, but it had been upgraded to another level.

There was card tables, a pool hall, a dance floor, open bar that serviced drinks, no alcohol of course, and an upstairs diner. It was just like an adult club, but for teens.

"Hey, June! What's up?

"June! Girl, you came to senior ditch day?"

"Not miss girly girly! We really about to turn up.

"Hi" June replied to everyone she passed.

Why are all of my peers acknowledging me? It's not like I'm that stuck up, or nerdy not to come to ditch day! Am I that lame? I mean, really! They thought I wouldn't come? Junes facial expression said everything without her speaking a word.

"Erica! Why y'all didn't tell me about senior ditch day?" June asked one of the most popular cheerleaders in the school.

"Girl, you be book bound, and to yourself. Me personally, I thought Stephanie would've told you. She the one started the rumor of all the seniors meeting at Polo's anyway."

"Well, we don't talk like that no more."

"Yeah, I heard." Replies Erica. "She told me how you came over her house, and she handled yo ass." June just start laughing, this chick never quits.

"Erica, please! She could only wish that was the truth. Have you seen Frank?"

"Yeah, he's back there in the pool hall."

"Thanks girl!"

"Yep!" Erica replies. "We stoppin at the movies, and then the south side roller rank, after we leave here. Two hours at each place, if you down."

"Okay, I'm down." June replied, as she laid eyes on Frank.

She got scared to walk in the pool hall, but needed the information.

"Hey guys!"

"What's up June?"

"Hi, Frank!" June spoke to Frank directly.

"Hey, girl! You lookin cute today. Let me see child. Okay! Bubble gum pink pants, all white halter top, with yo Jordan 12 Retro's, and the Tory Burch shoulder bag. I see yea boo."

June just smiled. Getting a gay boys dress approval is like making the cover of Elle.

"Thank you! Frank, but listen. You got a minute?"

"Yeah! Girl, anything for one of the smartest bitches in the school."

Frank waved off to his friends as he followed in June's direction. June went upstairs to the balcony where there was some kind of peace, and quiet.

"Damn, girl! What's so important, we have to go on the damn roof, honey!"

"Frank, I just wanted to talk to you about Terrell."

"Oh, shit honey! Not Terrell?"

"Yes, Frank! Terrell! I wanted to speak to you in private, and since I didn't have your number, this is the only thing I could think of.

"Oh! No, boo! Everything cool?" says Frank. "I'm just trying to figure out what that has to do with me?" Frank knew exactly where this conversation was going, but wasn't about to volunteer any of his information.

"Well, Frank. I did see you, and Terrell at the hospital a couple of weeks ago.

"Naw boo! You ain't seen Frank in no hospital!"

The waitress brings Frank his coke, and walks away laughing. Frank seems to bring amusement everywhere he goes with his appearance alone.

He stands at about 5'7; big hazel eyes, contacts of course, slim as a pencil, and can dress anyone under the rug. He had on some Aeropostale khaki jeans, with a black tank top. Which had female lips halted open, and a gold grill, as teeth. To top it off, the lips had a grown on them, and on the bottom of the shirt it read: Hood Bitch. He has a dark skin complexion, and extremely white teeth. His smile can make any women jealous, and he knew it. He is the epitome of a fine gay man, to say the least.

When dealing with Frank everyone knows to come correct, or don't come at all. Hints, way Frank only gave the waitress a fake smile back composing his words, so he wouldn't get tossed out of Polo's yet again.

"Frank, come on. I know who, and what I saw. I just need to know the truth. My feelings are at stake. Please Frank!"

"June, like I said, I don't know what the hell you are talking about. So, if you will, boo! I have to go."

"Wait, Frank!"

Frank just jumps up and, places his coke money under the salt shaker then walks away. June sits back down in complete discuss.

Well, that got me no where. My only other option is to go talk to Terrell.

June hands the waitress her, and Franks money, but notice a note beside Franks five dollar bill. **Here's my number (810)335-6874. Meet me tonight, we'll talk at five.**

June just smiles with joy. I thought he was dawdling, and didn't want to talk.Why would I be happy that Frank wants to meet with me about my boyfriend? This completely sucks, but at the least I'll get the answers I need before I face Terrell.

June returns downstairs with the rest of her peers, with the intent to follow throughout the plans of ditch day, but couldn't keep her composure, and wanted to see Terrell.

When leaving Polo's, June couldn't help but hope her eyes did deceive her, and it all was a lie.

I really hope I'm over thinking this, and Frank is just overzealous with Terrell. I mean, we all know Frank is over the top anyway. Terrell can't be gay, or bisexual. I love him too much to lose him, before I have him.

June left to get her mind prepare for Frank, but decided to go see Terrell. She had to back tract throughout several text messages to see if she still had his address in here phone, as to where he invited her over, but of course she couldn't come.

"Hi, Mr. Brown. How are you?"

"I can't complain," replied Mr. Brown.

"I'm here to see Terrell, if that's okay."

"Sure honey! I'm sorry, where are my manners? Come on in. Would you like a drink?"

"No, sir!" Replies June.

"I would paw paw." A little girl comes running from the back, and stands directly in front of June.

"Okay, pumpkin! I think I can handle that."

So, this is Ally, June thought. She is so beautiful, and little. Her little puff balls. She ain't no taller than 2 feet. She's just so adorable with a shirt that reads: I know I'm cute.

"Hi, I'm June, and you are?" June kneels down to Ally's level, and reaches out her hand, but Ally slaps it away.

"No! Like this." Ally says, and takes June's hand, and place's it in a high five position.

"Oh, I'm so sorry." Replies June with laughter.

Mr. Brown comes out the kitchen, and hands Alley her drink. "Here Ally, and leave June alone. I'm sorry June. I've just been busy all day. The nanny's off, Terrell's off to therapy, I'm working from home today, and playing with little Ally, all at the same time. Damn, that's right! I invited you in, and Terrell is in therapy." Mr. Brown phone beeps. "Excuse me, I have to take this, give me one minute."

"Sure!" June replies. Then she sits on the floor to play more with Ally.

"Hey, little lady. Do you know your ABC's?"

"Yes, ma'am." Ally replies. "I know yours too."

June just couldn't contain her smile. She's so freaking cute. I would love to take her with me. She looks like both of them, the Browns and the Taylors. I see more of Terrell's father in her than Terrell. I mean, look at her! She's short, kind of chunky, naturally curly hair just like any other mixed child, but those eyes. Those eyes are going to be deadly. They're not hazel, or blue. They look like a mix of both. So, I know Terrell will pay, when she starts dating.

"Hey June!"

"Oh, Terrell! I was just... I mean… I wanted..."

"June, It's ok. Well, I see you have met my daughter. I mean.... Ally."

"Yes! Terrell, and she is so adorable."

June gets up off the floor, and walks over to the gray suede couch, to help Terrell prop his foot up. Terrell I just wanted to talk to you about the letter I left in your phone.

"Daddy!"

"Yes, dear!"

Both Terrell and Darnell responded to Ally's call. June thought, did I miss something, but chose to mind her business.

"Sometimes she calls Darnell dad. Meaning, paw paw!" Terrell replied in full embarrassment, trying to refrain from telling the true.

"I understand. Will we be able to talk privately about the letter, and why..." before June could say Franks name Mrs. Brown entered the room, placing her keys on the key holder.

"Hi, June! How are you?"

"I'm doing great, Mrs. Brown. I just came to check on Terrell."

"How sweet is that, and may I ask how school is going. Any nursing offers yet?"

June just smiled. "No, ma'am, but if you can give me some great referrals, I'll really appreciate it."

"Sure thing, honey. I will do anything for my future daughter in law."

Mrs. Brown walks past Terrell, and pats him on the shoulder. I'll give you two some space, so y'all can clear some things up. Mrs. Brown walks into the kitchen to start lunch for Ally, picking up toys along the way, as Ally followed.

"Terrell, listen! I really want to know what's up with you and Frank?" June whispered, trying to be as quite as possible, so Mrs. Brown couldn't hear her.

"June I really can't talk about that right here, right now. But, in about a week, I'll be able to get out again, and we can sit down for dinner."

"No! That's not cool with me. I've been waiting for this relationship to grow into something for months, and you want me to wait. That's just not fair!" June though, but just looked down at her phone for the time, and noticed a missed text from Frank, that reads: **Just come now. 2:33 P.M.**

"Oh, Terrell I have to go, but thanks! I really enjoyed seeing you."

"Um, Ok! I'll see you later, I guess!" June grab her keys, and bolted towards the door.

"Before you go June, will you come here?" June walks over to Terrell, and he pulls her down by the hand to bring her down to his level.

"Thanks June, I really mean it!"

He gives her a small kiss on the lips, looks her square in the eyes, and begins to tear up before stating the obvious.

"I can't stress enough how much that meant to me. When you came to the hospital, really help me understand how much you care for me. Well, I might as well go ahead and tell you, I love you too!"

June eyes widen with shock. "You heard me? You heard everything I said?"

"Yes! I heard everyone. I just couldn't respond." Terrell replies, never taking his eyes off June.

"I have to go!" June jumps up, and excuses herself. Letting her own self out the door. Terrell couldn't chase after her, or react like he wanted to. He just laid his head back, and embraced Ally, who jumped in his lap.

16

June pulled up to the Shallow Creek. A beautiful park where people met for dates, events, and even weddings. There were waterfalls, palm trees, and even a walking trail. Big lakes that people could go fishing in, and even a place for beach activities. Frank was already sitting on the bench overlooking the water.

"Miss Bitch, how are you?"

"I'm making it Frank. You will not believe the weekend I had." They both kiss each other on the cheeks as they sat down watching the jet skiers pass through.

"Well, that's why we are here, to talk boo. So, What's up?"

"Frank, let's start with this you and Terrell thing. What's up with that? Did y'all hook up? Did y'all kiss, or am I diving too deep into this. Please let me know something."

"Ok! Boo, we just go take this slow. What happened, was not what you think."

"What should I think?" Replies June. "I'm very confused on why you were kissing him on the forehead? Why you were pacing back and forth, and why you was even there?" June begins to feel hurt, but held back her tears.

"June! I understand, but me and Terrell are nothing. Well, not to him anyway. Let me just break everything down for you, and explain way things are the way they are."

"Me, Terrell, and Stephanie was all hanging out one night. Somehow, she purchases some beer. So, we drinking, and we were in her apartment dancing, playing games, and having a good time. Stephanie started dancing with me. Let me first make this clear. I had mixed feeling about my sexuality then, and I sure wasn't about to share it with anyone until I know for sure myself. So, we having a good time, and Stephanie kissed me. I didn't feel no kind of way, but Terrell did. He pushed me out the way, grabbed her by the waist, and kissed her. That's when I really started liking Terrell, and his aggressiveness. Things kept getting heavy between them, or should I say us. So, I was like, yo let's have a threesome. I'm thinking no one will take me seriously. Terrell, of course just started laughing, and dap me up. Steph didn't say much of anything. She just took another drink, hit the blunt, and walked back to her room."

June just looked disturbed, and glanced down at her phone.

Hey June!	**1:30 P.M.**
Hi Terrell, how are you?	**1:30 P.M.**
I just wanted to talk to you!	**1:34 P.M.**
What's up?	**1:36 P.M.**
Did I scare you when I said I love you?	**1:40 P.M.**

. . . .

"June! What's up? You really go sit here, and text someone while I'm trying to give you the 411 on what happen with me and Terrell."

"I'm sorry it's my mother. She is very controlling, and needs to know what I'm doing at all times. So, I have to keep her posted. I'm sorry love. I'm listening"

"It's cool! Where was I? So, we drinking and dancing. Terrell and Stephanie were basically getting it in. I asked for a threesome, and they both seemed shocked, but didn't seem resistant."

June, I really do love you!   **2:00 PM**

Terrell, I really don't know what to say! I love you too!!!!!

But?   **2:00 PM**

But??? What does what mean?   **2:05 PM**

"So, girl! I was like, let's do this." Frank replied. "So, we go into the bedroom, and Stephanie excused herself, and

255

went in the bathroom. Terrell began to take off his shirt, and shorts. I couldn't do nothing but stare, and I mean, stare hard. His abs was extremely firm, and I completely loved that he had back muscles. I was drooling like a wet puppy in heat. Girl! It was so unreal. Of course, he got a little uncomfortable cause he was like, *"Damn dude, the fuck you looking at."* June all I could say was um, and nothing else."

Frank and June both started laughing with the understanding that they both have seen Terrell topless. Frank continued the conversation with a smile on his face reliving each moment.

"Then Stephanie brings her rumple ass out the bathroom, which I should've of locked her in, but after looking in her direction to see what she was doing. I turned my head away from Terrell. Honey! When I looked back, I was standing on the other side of the bed. Terrell was standing there completely nude. Yes, honey! Nude, stroking his dick waiting! Okay! Let me say that again, waiting honey! Long, and strong. June just smiled, and joined hands with Frank as he insisted on the playful act.

"Oh my goodness, Frank! What did you do next."

"My lips dropped to the floor, boo. I mean, what could I do, but get undressed as fast as I could, and climb in the bed."

June, do you not love me?   **2:10 P.M.**

Of course, baby! I just wanted to know, why Frank was in your room kissing your forehead?   **2:11 P.M.**

I couldn't tell you that, I'm pissed off about it myself, that he was even in there.   **2:11 P.M.**

What can you tell me? Because if we're moving on, I really need to know.   **2:15 P.M.**

First off, nothing happened with me and him. I am not gay, but I just don't want to say, because I feel like I've already put you through too much.   **2:16 P.M.**

Well! What happen? Trust, I can handle it.   **2:17 P.M.**

....

"So, bitch! We got in the bed. Me and Stephanie both got under the covers. She was going down to perform oral on him, while I did her was the plan. Honey! It went the other way around. I just couldn't help myself. I couldn't restrain myself any longer, and Stephanie ass was so drunk, she kept falling over."

"Frank! No, please say it isn't so. Please, tell me that didn't happen?"

"Yes, trick, and you better not tell nobody. Terrell to this day still don't know it was me who made him cum in five minutes. Ok bitch!"

June just froze solid. "Man, I'm... "I'm just... I can't believe that happened. Frank, did that really happen?"

"Girl! I been gay ever since. Do you hear me?"

June couldn't reply. She could barely move. Her mouth stayed open, but not one single word came out. So, Frank continued.

"I stayed, and watched them both get it in. I was adding a hand here, and a finger there. But, me! Myself, I couldn't complete the task. I wanted Terrell for myself so bad at that point, but I had to go. So, I just left. I couldn't tell you if they noticed, or not they just kept going."

"Wow! June replied. Umm, I'm at a loss for words. I mean, did you ever talk to him, or Stephanie after?"

"Hell! No." Frank replied. "I basically exposed myself, after me, and Stephanie kicked it for a minute. And, I only feel comfortable telling you because I know you ain't go tell know body, but as you can see, I'm very comfortable with my sexuality now.

Well, Terrell I'm waiting?   **2:20 P.M.**

Ok! Please don't be mad, but I've hooked up with

Stephanie more than that one time.   2:20 P.M.

Really? Terrell!   2:25 P.M.

Yes! I'm going to be truthful with you about everything,

because I want you to forgive me, and we really give our

love a try.   2:27 P.M.

Ok! What else? You said everything,

 Like there's more.   2:28 P.M.

It was a threesome, and Frank was there. Nothing

happened with me and Frank, it was me and Stephanie,

who, um... Fu#ked. He just watched   2:30 P.M.

Okay! I'ma call you in ten. K.   2:31 P.M.

Wow! Really, after I just... Bye   2:31 P.M.

......

"Frank, did you'll ever hook back up one on one, or
was that the last time?"

"Girl! Terrell and Stephanie just stop talking for whateva reason, except for when you came to this school. You know, Terrell can't stand Stephanie. Last I heard, they still bumping heads. I know cause I still keep tabs on my boo." Frank became overly excited at the thought of thinking about Terrell. "And, before you ask, yes! That's Terrell's baby. Damn! Now that I think about it, they had to hook up some other time to have had a baby. Miss thing nasty now tho. They said that she be with anybody that gives her attention."

"Frank. You can't base your opinion on what other people say."

"Girl, please! These girls want to be thots now days." Frank and June both started laughing understanding the truth behind that statement.

"Why you are defending someone who said they go whoop that ass at graduation?"

"What?"

"Yes, honey! She is planning on beating that ass during your graduation speech."

"How do you know?"

"She told Marie, and you know Marie my baby. So, you know she go tell me everything."

Junes whole demeanor changed. "You know what Frank, let me go. I'ma put an end to this now."

"Oh, shit! Um, bitch! What you about to go do?"

"Put some thots in check."

"Bitch! Know you not? Can I come witcha?"

"Come on!"

"Aw shit! Oh hell yah! You about to beat that ass again?"

They both make their way to June's car, and head up the highway.

"Honey! Let me put my seat belt on, this about to be a ride."

June knew that this was completely out of her character. But, Frank boosted her ego enough to at least ride through. June just road around town until she spotted Stephanie and Marie at the 7 11.

"You really want to fight this ghetto chick again, or just see what happens at graduation." Frank asked after sticks his head out the window yelling. "Heyyy bitch, and waving his hand at Stephanie."

"Shit, now. I got to turn around."

June though to herself did I just cuss? Who am I becoming? Frank pulled his head back in the window.

"They right there! Where you gon? Pull a U-turn, so we can see what these chicks talking bout."

"I am, give me a second."

"Why you sound scared, Bitch? Don't be scared."

"I'm not scared Frank." June replied, as she took a deep breath when pulling into the 7 11. Knowing she wasn't scared, but didn't like confrontation.

Man! I really hate drama, but I'll have to face this girl yet again. Let me get this settled, once and for all.

"Damn! June. You gon get out the car?"

"Yes! Can I put the car in park first?" Already exhausted, she jumped out the car already in defense mode ready to stand her ground.

"What's up Marie?"

"Hey June. I'ma chill over here with Frank, and give y'all some room to talk."

Stephanie just stood with her hands behind her back already balled up in a fist ready for something to pop off.

"Listen! I didn't come here to fight. I came to clear the air."

"Bitch, who said I wanted to clear the air with you."

"Dang! Stephanie, can we be grown about this for just one minute."

"One minute, and go!"

"Well, I just wanted to know about the threesome, and is that when you got pregnant?"

Stephanie just looked up at Frank with complete disguise.

"How you go tell our secret Frank?"Stephanie yells.

"What secret?" Marie replies.

"Oh! No, trick. Don't come for me? I ain't June. I'll beat dat ass first, then ask questions."

"Stephanie! Look, I just want things to be leveled, so we can go our separate ways."

"Bitch! You ruined my life, and expect me to just walk away. Please! Get yo life! I'll see you when I see you."

"Well, I do believe your life was already ruined before you even meet me, but whatever!

"Alright, now!" Frank yelled out. "It's getting juicy."

Stephanie was about to reach back, and slap June in midair, but the manger at 7 11 told them to leave the property. He didn't allow drama, and wasn't about to start.

June watched over her shoulder as she pulled out her keys, and walked to her car. She glanced at the time as she jumped in knowing it was best to call her mother, but she couldn't get over the fact of who she was becoming.

What am I doing here? Who am I? This is not my behavior. I'm usually classy, and mature. The old June would've just walked away, or not even played a part to this madness. Why have I let this environment change me, or should I say Stephanie. I've got to do better.

June drove away, and headed home where she could get some peace. Leaving behind Frank, whom she forgot rode with her.

17

Clay walked in from work to a home cooked meal, and a very clean home. There wasn't a thing out of place, and Dawn was grooving with her headsets waiting for June to come home.

"Dawn, that box wasn't packed for show." Clay said, letting his authority be known.

"Clay, I don't care what it was packed for. You ain't about to do nothing, but talk a good game. We had sex, it was good, and now we back at our regular flow, come taste this sauce."

"Where is June?"

"Getting out of school! Why?"

"Alright boys y'all can come in."

Mr. Avery ordered the officers in, and asked the movers to remove all the things from June's room, and if

Mrs. Avery acted out of order to remove her too. Dawn turned her homemade Alfredo sauce off, and stepped directly in Clay's face.

"What the hell are you doing?" Clay just walked pass her without saying a word.

"Clay, answer my question." She cried, as she chased him down.

"Ma'am, I'm going to need you to calm down, unless you want to be removed." The officer replied, standing at attention, with one hand on his hip, and the other in midair.

"Y'all ain't gone remove me from shit."

"Ma'am, we are not playing. I will physically remove you from this situation. Now we are just here to make sure that the move is orderly."

Mr. Avery just shook his head in agreement, and begins to smile.

"Clay, please answer me!"

"Dawn, listen! I ain't got that kind of time. I tried to put everything out on the table, but your other lover Lace, let me know exactly where we stand."

"Please! Let's just have dinner with Lace, and we can clear everything up from there."

"Where? At 1424." Clay replied, begin very sarcastic.

"Clay! Can we please just hash this out?"

"You set up the meeting, but that still don't have an effect on what's taking place today. You and your damn brat are out of here.

Dawn just grabbed her purse, and headed to the door. "After 16 years she's your brat too. By the way, did you tell the police you had a thing for your own daughter?"

Clay didn't even respond to Dawn's comment. He just went on with his motive of getting Dawn out of the house. "Hold on, my dear! I think you're forgetting something."

Dawn just looked up in despair, "What Clay! What am I forgetting?"

"The keys baby!"

"My keys?" Says Mrs. Avery, in honest confusion, to his vague demand.

"Yes! Your keys, not only to the house, but the car as well."

"Clay, how am I suppose to get around?"

"You know that Honda Accord you had when I met you?"

"Yeah! So."

"Oh, it's been in storage baby, just in case this happened. Don't worry, I kept up the maintenance, so it's set to go."

Clay tossed the keys in Dawn's direction, but they just fell to the floor. Dawn bent over to pick them up, and she could no longer hold back her tears.

"Don't cry now." Clay replied. "You weren't crying when you were doing your dirty."

"Don't worry, Clay. You'll get yours, trust me. One way or another, you got one coming.

Dawn left out the house furiously. Why am I even trying to make amends with this bastard. When he's been making my daughter feel uncomfortable. I've got to call Lace. So, I can get a place for me, and June to stay.

Dawn started her Honda, and it sounded better than when she originally had it. It was full of gas, and ready to go. She followed the U-Haul truck, and called John Lace.

"Who in the hell, Puts out a woman, and her child? Then, Clay had the nerve to save my car, as if he knew this would happen. Him and his insecurities are the reason I step out in the first place."

"Dawn, is that you?"

"Yes, Lace." Dawn called weeping.

271

"He did what?" Lace replied in anger! "Where are you now?"

"I don't know, I'm following the U-Haul truck to see where they are placing my things. Will I be able to meet you at your house?"

"Of course, Dawn. Just give me a few good minutes, and I'll come get you.

"No, I'll just get the U-Haul to meet me at your house in an hour."

They both hang up the phone realizing the urgency. Dawn flagged down the U-Haul to let them know that there was a change of plans, and needed their time with some assistance. Lace rolled over, and taps his lady friend on the shoulder.

"Hey, boo. I'ma have to ask you to leave a little earlier than usual. Something very important has come up, and I must get things prepared."

"Well, that's cool." She replied. "I have to go back home, and check on Terrell anyway. Will I see you later?"

"I don't know right now. I hate to say it, but this might be the last encounter to our little quick pick me ups."

"I'm ok with that. Although, I know I'm going to miss King, but hey! Family comes first."

They both started laughing with an adult understanding of their agreement, and who King was.

"Call me later at the office if you can."

"Ok, Babe!" Mrs. Aldis gave Lace a kiss, and headed out the back door like any other day.

Lace stood up, and begins to get the house in order. Changing sheets, cleaning closets, bathrooms, and sweeping floors. He then walks in his special room where he always kept the door closed. Lace stood still for a minute, and took a deep breath. Once he entered the room. The smell of paint still remained fresh, as if he just finished that day. The pink and cream walls almost brought him to tears.

Standing beside the full size bed, he begins rubbing the pink lace sheets that were custom made with the name *June*! There was a small baby picture of June on her princess dresser, from when Dawn sent it to him for his personal records. He dreamed of this day. And, although he gave the situation a little push, he was overly excited.

All these years I've waited for this moment. Deep down I wasn't ready to be a father, because I just didn't know if I could handle what all came with it. Lord, knows, I'm ready now. Lace smile grew bigger, as the doorbell rung.

"Coming!" He yelled, as he threw the rest of the pillows on the bed, and ran to the door with pure enthusiasm. He swung the door open, and was greeted with a surprise.

"Please, put the gun down, and relax." Lace said, slowly walking backwards with his hands in the air, and the gun to his face. "Who are you? Why are you here?"

"Don't worry about who I am. Are you John Lace?"

"Sir! You pulled the gun out, and pointed it directly in my face, before knowing who I was. So, I want to know who you are? And what business do you have here?"

"You sure do have a tight, tough for someone who has a gun pointed to their face." The man replied. "Now get down on the floor." John Lace followed orders.

"Why are you here, and what have I done to you?" The man took the glock 9, and whacked Lace across the head.

"Now, that should hush you up!"

"Damn, man!" Lace replied, placing his hand over his head falling completely to the floor. The man took a long thick rope out of his back pocket, and hog tied Lace.

"Now, I got a couple questions for you. Who is Aldis Brown to you, and why was she here?"

"What man?" Mr. Lace replied. Another whack from the nine crossed John's head, as a result of not answering the question.

"Again, this is my last time asking, or I'm popping! Who is Aldis Brown to you?"

Lace hesitated, then replied. "Aldis is just a friend."

"Wrong answer." Pop! The gun fires, but the bullet didn't released.

"Shit! The safety is on. Damn! I forgot. Ok, let's try this again. Is Aldis just your mistress?"

"Yes, man! Damn! I swear nothing more, nothing less. We are good friends that hook up sometimes. What's it to you?"

The gravel of a car, pulling into the yard caught the gentleman off guard.

"I'm not go kill you today, just know this is not the end." The man popped the rope with the scissors he took out his back pocket, and walked out. He was so calm and collective that Mrs. Avery couldn't tell that there was trouble.

"Hi, there Mrs.Lady! How are you?" The man asked, with the brightest smile as if nothing happened.

"I'm great Terrell! What are you doing here? How do you know John?"

"Oh, he's just an old friend of the family. That's all!"

"Well, I'm glad to see you doing better!"

"Yes, ma'am! The therapy worked wonders. My mother hired a personal trainer, so I can heal faster. Or, at least stand on my own two feet." They both start laughing, like two old friends catching up.

"You tell your mom I said hello."

"Yes, ma'am!"

"I'll give an update to June, so she'll know how well you're doing."

They turned their heads to the door as Lace swung it open, to tell Dawn to beware. But, he didn't say a word when he saw Dawn was comfortable with who she was talking to.

"I have to go, but you take care." Mrs. Avery walked up the crosswalk, while John Lace ran to her side. The closer he got, the more nerves, she got.

"Lace, are you ok?

"Yeah"

"That was just Terrell. Are you good? What happen?" Lace didn't respond, he just watched Terrell drive off. "Hello, what the hell happened, and why would Terrell be over here?"

Lace just grab Dawn by the arm. "Don't worry about that. What did he say to you?"

"What did who say? Terrell!" Answering her own question. "Oh! He just wanted to know how I was doing. I know his mother."

"So, that's Terrell?" Replied Lace. "It all makes sense now. I get it." Lace couldn't say anything, but now he knows why Terrell was at his place.

"Did he do this to you?" Dawn noticed the gash in his head. "Did he put his hands on you?"

"No! Don't worry about me, I'm fine! Just like he told you I'm just an old friend of the family, and he just came to check on me."

"Oh, ok! I was just being sure, because I can handle that for you." John Lace just smiled, and wrapped his arms around Dawn's waist. Remembering why he fell in love with her in the first place.

"Let's go in the house, and talk this over before June gets here.

18

June pulled up to what was once her home, and put her unrecognized pin code in. The yard was full of movers and U-Haul trucks, but she still didn't understand what was going on. When one of the movers rode out, she pulled right in, and parked.

What is going on? She thought, as she put down her bags, and walked up the long driveway. She begins to wiggle her key, but it didn't work. The door locks are changed to? Did we get evicted? What is going on?

June started walking away before a young man stopped her.

"Hey pretty lady!" The young mover approached her, as she simply kept walking.

"Hey! Is there something I can help you with."

"No!" June replied, as she gave him that leave me the alone face.

"Well, Miss Lady since you is so pretty. I will go ahead and tell you what's going on. The home owner threw out his girlfriend, and her little brat of a daughter, as he put it."

She looked at the mover, puzzled yet questionable! Before she could respond the mover eventually got it.

"Damn, your the brat."

"Yep!"

"Listen! I'm sorry, I didn't know."

"It's ok!" She said, still in motion.

"Hey!"

What does he want now? She thought, and paused with her hand on her hip.

"I can give you the address to where they dropped off your mothers belongings."

June walked closer to the mover for more information.

"Sure, thanks a lot!"

The mover handed over the information. He apologized once more, because he felt bad about his behavior.

"Thanks again," says June.

"No Problem."

Back in her car, she puts the address in her GPS.

This place is twenty minutes from home. What happen? I hope mom didn't find out what Clay has been doing to me! I was going to tell her, but I was waiting for the right time. I wonder if they got into another fight. Clay can be very irrational at times.

She pulled up to a big blue house with all white panels, and a white picket fence. The grass was green, and freshly cut.

This can't be it! I mean it's a nice house, but it's sure not what I'm used to. Where is the garage, the pool, the back deck. All I see is a yard with a child's swing set in the back. I see the U-Haul truck, and a gray Honda in the driveway, but that's not my mother's car.

June gets out, and holds on to the stairwell, then heard moaning coming from the living room.

I'll come back, they sound a little too busy up in there. Before June could walk away a man yelled from the door crack.

"Who the fuck are you?" When June turned back to see who was talking to her, all she could see was the barrow of a gun.

"Umm, I'm... I'm...," before she could answer, all she felt was wet fluids running down her legs.

"Lace, who is it, and why are you pointing that gun?"

"Mom?" Yelled June.

"Lace, my goodness, get that damn gun out my child's face. Have you lost yo mind?"

"June!"

Lace lowered the gun, walked in the house, and reached for his pants. June didn't move, her feet wouldn't allow her to. She just stood there in tears, as she yelled her mother's name. Mrs. Avery walked out with nothing but a long T-shirt, and her undergarment.

"Baby! Come in. We have a lot going on, and we need to talk."

Pulling June in Dawn showed her to the bathroom, and told her to take a shower. June followed her mother's directions, as she never took her eyes off Lace.

"Mother, who is that man? Where have I seen him before, and why are we even here?"

"June! Just get in the shower, we will discuss all those things when you come back downstairs."

"Mother, I have no clothes here"

"Honey, all those boxes you're stepping over, is our stuff. I'll find you something, don't worry."

"Mom, please don't leave me."

"You'll be okay, honey. He just didn't know who you were."

June's face said it all, as she followed orders from her mother. Once out of the shower, she put on the clothes her mother laid out, and then rushed downstairs.

"Okay, mom who is he?" June grabs her mother by the arms, as she pulls her to the side. Feeling very scared, and discombobulated, she would not leave her mother's side.

Lace walked into the dining area to be greeted by Dawn and June.

"Dawn, I can handle this, just give us a little one on one time.

"NO! Mother, No! I don't know him. Do not leave me alone with this man. For goodness sake he pulled a gun out on me.

"Trust me, it's okay."

"It's okay baby girl, I can understand. For starters, I'm Lace. Well, John Lace, and I am...

"Please spit it out, you're who my father?" June started laughing, but they gave no response.

"Wait! That was a joke. Ha ha. Are you my father for real?" Dawn just stood quiet to June's reaction, and John had no words. "Someone please say something. We all are the adults here! Are you my father?"

"Yes. I'm your birth father. Here's the birth certificate to prove it. I know this may have caught you off guard. And, it definitely wasn't the formal way for use to meet, but I am your father. I haven't been in your life peer say, but I've been here."

"What the hell does that mean?"

"June, are you crazy, don't speak to your father in that tone. Now you apologize. When did you start using that kind of language, have you lost your damn mind?"

"My father, my father! No! My father lives twenty minutes away from here. That's my dad. Yeah, he's a dick, but he's the only dick I know. But, I don't know this clown."

June grabs her bags, and storm out the dining room. Throwing down the birth certificate Lace gave her. But Dawn wouldn't let her leave.

"Apologize, right now young lady. This is the very reason I've tried to keep a tight leash on you. So you wouldn't end up like this."

"Like what mother? Like one of your reckless clients. Who don't give a damn what their parents think. Well, guess what mother, I'm there. I don't have time for this bullshit, I have graduation tomorrow, and I'm going home."

Dawn grabs June by the arm before she knew it, and June yanked away.

"Who do you think you're talking to like that? And, this is your home, now. So, you better straighten up, and act right, before I get that act right, and you know exactly what I'm talking about."

"What are you going to do, whoop me? Well, those days are over. I'm so tired of you trying to control me, mother. I am a grown now, and have my own life to live. I have to go."

Dawn was floored. She never heard June talk to her with such disrespect. Lace just stood with a look of disappointment, as June walked out the door.

"This is not exactly how I thought things would go."

"Neither did I," said Dawn as she chased June down.

"Dawn, just let her go. She's hurting right now, which I can understand."

"But, did you hear how she was talking to me? Like hell."

"Yes, honey. I know. But, trust me she'll come around. It's a lot to take in, in one day. You should understand that with the line of work you do."

Dawn and Lace both stood on the porch, as they watched June get in her car and pull out the driveway, rolls her window down, and yell. "I'll be home when you're done here."

June speeds down the road with no regard to how she treated her mother.

My whole life has spiraled out of control. I don't know where I live, graduation is tomorrow, I haven't seen Terrell nor has he made contact with me. I'm sure it's been about a week since we spoke, with his gay ass. My mom is a thot, and at this moment I feel like beating Stephanie's ass just because, and this John Lace guy can completely kiss my balls.

June pulls back up to Clay's home. All the movers were gone, but there were a squad of police cars, and ambulances everywhere. Clay's car was in the driveway at this time, but it still looked like a crime scene.

What now. June asked herself I can't leave one house where there's drama, without coming to another.

June jumps out of her car, and tried to run up the driveway where she's met by Clay.

"Clay, are you okay?

"Ma'am, I'ma need you to step back." The officers replied. June could only get a flashback of what happen to Terrell in that instant.

"No! Let her in," Clay replied.

"Clay are you okay?"

"Yeah, I'm good. I don't know what's going on around here lately. But, some boy has gone on a rampage. He was running around the house screaming your name, and shooting a gun. Talking about how, he can't wait to see you, and how you got him fucked up. So, I had to put him in his place real quick. I let him know, he not gone run up on me, and think it's ok."

"Who is it? You didn't kill him did you?"

"No! He's right over there, a little bruised up, but he's good. The neighbors called the cops of course, and they brought along the ambulance."

June walked over to the squad car to see who it was. Completely caught off guard, she could only speak his name.

"Frank! Why would he do this?" Clay, walked beside June.

"Do you know this cat, because if not, I'm go press charges to the fullest."

"Yes, I know him." June replies, and please don't do that. I know you hate me, and mom at the moment, but Clay, he's a friend of mine."

"I'll think about it, and I don't hate you." Clay places his hands on June's shoulder.

June didn't even reply. She just watched as they drove away with Frank, wondering why the heck Frank would do this.

"I mean, really. Has he lost his damn mind?" June said, as she looked Clay face to face. "Clay, can I stay here tonight? I have no where else to go."

"Sure, baby doll, and when did you start cussing?"

"I'm sorry Clay, but it's been a terrible day."

"It's okay, I was going to suggest that anyway. It's too late to be out, and don't you graduate tomorrow.

"Yeah, I do!"

June just walked away, knowing this couldn't go well. Following her intuition, she got in her car, and left. Riding the roads in circles, she didn't know which way to turn. Before she knew it, she pulled into Terrell's yard, and pulled out her phone.

Hey Bae!	10:30P.M.
Damn girl! I haven't heard	
from you in days.	10:32P.M.
I know stress!! Smh	10:32P.M.
Stress, what's up?	
I thought I did something wrong.	10:34P.M.
Outside your place!	10:36P.M.
Stop playing!!	10:37P.M.
I really am!	10:37 P.M.

......

Terrell didn't even reply back, but June could see where the curtains were moving. With a complete smile on her face, June couldn't do nothing, but think about the time they were laying in what she thought was his bed. By the time she looked up Terrell was standing at her door.

"Open the door." Says Terrell, as he pulls on the handle.

June did as told, and he pulls her straight out the car, and into his arms.

"Terrell, please!" Replied June, knowing she needed every bit of his love.

"Girl, stop! Let me have you for a minute." June just smiled, and gave in.

"Park your car behind the house, and please stay the night with me!"

"I can't graduation is tomorrow."

June still wrapped in Terrell's arms, knowing that she was staying, because she had no where else to go, but didn't want to give Terrell no predetermined ideas.

"You're staying!"

Terrell got in her cream Prius, and pulled it right next to his new all black Aston Martin.

"They finally got you a new car, and a good one at that."

"Do you like it?"

"Of course, who wouldn't!"

"Okay, be quiet, everyone's sleeping, or locked in their rooms. So, we'll be good! Besides, mom would rather me be in the house, instead of the streets."

"And Stephanie?" She replied sarcastically!

"I almost called you something. Now be quiet, and come upstairs." They both tread softly to Terrells room, with giggles and laughs.

"Boy, this ain't know room, It's a studio apartment. I would never leave this place. You got, hardwood flooring, your own bathroom, a king size bed, and a refrigerator. Dang, boy! You got a basketball rim in your room!" June was in complete amazement. "Can I be your roommate?"

Terrell smiled, "Come over here."

"No!"

"No! What the hell does that mean?" Terrell asked with a smile on his face. "I got you right where I want you now."

"It means exactly what I said."

Terrell Just laughed, got up from his bed, and walked over to the half court where June was standing. Terrell walked right past her, but was so close she could feel his heart beat.

"What are you doing?" replied June, as she smiled, and looked into his big hazel eyes.

"Getting the remote! A brother can't watch Tv in his own room?"

She just started laughing, as Terrell pushed several buttons, but the TV didn't come on.

"I thought you were watching Tv?"

"Relax!" Terrell says, as the radio comes on, and the lights dim a little low.

"Oh, hell No! You ain't about to get me, and turn that down so your parents won't hear!"

"June come over here? And you cussing now"

"No! June said, smiling from ear to ear.

"No! For real, I need to talk to you. Well, as a matter of fact, let's play some basketball." June's face said it all.

"Basketball? Dude, your parents will hear us."

"No, they won't. My dad had my room custom-made. These are silent doors, and walls. So, I can practice anytime. Day or night, it's called, training."

"I don't believe you."

"You don't believe me?"

"I do, but I just don't see your parents doing that, as hands on, as your parents are. No! Way. How would they know what you're doing in here."

"They don't, but to some degree they trust me. Wait! I'll show you."

Terrell screamed at the top of his lungs. "Yoooo!!"

They both waited. "See, nothing. I'll do you one better."

Terrell told June to yell as loud as she could while he stepped outside the door. June instantly turned red!

"No! I can't do that.

"Just do it."

Laughter overtook her, and as soon as Terrell was about to re-enter Aldis walks past.

"Boy, what are you laughing at?" Terrell quickly pulled out his phone, and closed the door completely.

"I was texting Tony. Why? What's up ma?"

"Go in your room with that, and turn your music down your vents are open."

June just started laughing silently, and whispered "See I told you," as Terrell closed the door, and locked it.

Terrell jumped on his bed and closed his vent. They both started laughing, and playing half court dribble. Once he became tired, Terrell took a break and laid in the bed.

"So, how's the healing coming?"

"It's good, I still hurt from time to time, but at least my cast is off, but I still have therapy."

"That's just a part of the process. You'll be fine"

June was now completely comfortable in Terrell's presents. They cleared the air on everything possible, and begin to talk about their future. June was surprised at some of Terrells goals, because they all, wasn't centered around basketball. He actually started his own mentor group, and opened his own savings account from his allowance, and foundations he started.

"Terrell you have great goals. Why you never express any of these things in school?"

"Because no one never asked, June, I have plans set ahead for me and Ally. I just know it will take some time for me to get there, and basketball will be what pays for it."

June was so impressed she couldn't stop smiling. She scooted closer, and kissed Terrell on the cheek.

19

"Just relax, and lay your head back."

"I can't, Terrell! I'm too scared."

"We don't have to do this if you don't want to."

"I want to, I've never done this before, so I'm a little nervous. Besides, graduation is tomorrow, and we have to be there early. You're getting the valued sportsman award, and I have a speech to give."

"Oh shit! I got the athlete of the year award."

"Yes Hun!"

June just smiled knowing that Terrell has been waiting months for that award. And maybe with him thinking about that it will give her a little time to get herself together.

"I can respect you June. So, I'm ready when you're ready. No rush."

"Why do you respect me so much."

"Well, you've proved yourself strong, and loyal to me. I mean, you were at the hospital in my time of need, you are always checking on me, and I don't even want to talk about Stephanie. Another thing, is the fact that my parents like you. Which is a bonus to me, you stand strongly to your word, and lets not forget how damn attractive you are. You are truly a catch miss lady."

"Thank you, and please lets not talk about Stephanie." June replied. Can I ask you something?"

"What's up?"

"Do you really love me? I mean, like love me!"

Terrell didn't say anything, he just looked June in her eyes and gave her a slow stroke across her forehead. Then laid down, and looked up at the ceiling.

"Okay, I guess that's a No!" June got up, and started adjusting her hair.

Terrell jumped up! "Stay right there." June didn't move, and didn't ask any questions. Terrell ran to his drawer, and handed June a box that read Tiffany & Co.

What is this? June thought, but couldn't voice the words.

"June!" Terrell said, and repeated her name once more. "June! Ima need you to open that," as he laughed.

"Terrell." June replied, with a complete smile on her face. "I can't, I can't open this." June just handed Terrell the box back, and just laid back down with her back turned to Terrell.

"It's your graduation gift. I was going to wait until tomorrow at graduation, but you're here now."

Terrell rolled June over, and they just stared into each other eyes, for a minute. No words were spoken. The Weekend's Often was playing softly in the background, and the lighting was still dim. June reached over, and kissed him with tears in her eyes.

"Wait!" Terrell pushed her away, then asked. "Why are you crying?"

June didn't speak a word. She just kissed Terrell again, and begins to feel her emotions run all through her body. He didn't push her away this time, because this was a feeling he never felt himself. Lost in their emotions Terrell slowly removed June's shirt asking her permission first. June gave a head nod of yes, and Terrell did as told. Terrell than removed his own shirt, as June just sat with a nervous smile on her face.

"June, we don't have to do this. We can just lay, and hold each other." June stood up on the bed. "Girl! What are you doing?"

She removed her own pants, panties, and flopped back down. "Take me." They both started laughing, and got under the covers.

"Girl, you so silly."

He then cuffed her in his arms, and gives her the most passionate kiss they both ever experienced. She reached under the covers, into his shorts, and played with Terrell's manhood before picking up the Tiffany box on the night stand.

"So, what is it?"

"It's yours, open it." She pulled the white ribbon, and open the box. Terrell kissed June on the back of the neck, as tears fell from her eyes again.

"Terrell! How did you afford this?"

"Just put it on,"

She closed the box, and gave Terrell the biggest hug. More kisses were exchanged, and they both begin to feel gitty with excitement.

She laid on her back for a minute, as Terrell stared at her. The smiles on their faces couldn't be erased. While they were wondering if what they were experiencing was love.

June rolled on top of Terrell, popped her own bra, and let it fall to the floor.

"June, are you sure this is what you want to do?"

June slowly went under the covers, removed Terrells shorts, and pulled out his Johnson. She smiled at the strong feeling in her hand that she now kissed. The slow bob of her neck gave her a different feeling of excitement, and a moist feeling between her legs. Terrell smiled, arches his back, and placed one hand on her head, and the other to secure his place on the bed.

"June this feels way too good for this to be your first time."

June didn't do anything, but smiled as she felt his erection grow harder. She came up for air, and asked Terrell if he had any protection. Terrell reached in his night stand, and pulled out a box of condoms that read: magnum thins. Opening the new box, and removing one followed by the question he asked all night long.

"Are you sure you want to do this?"

"I'll put it on." June said, as she followed the instructions she remembered from sex Ed.

She looked at Terrell, and raised one eyebrow with a look of now did that answer your question. Once the condom was on. She climbed on top of him, and he stopped her.

"Wait! Since it's your first time, lay on your back, it won't hurt you as bad this way." June just looks amused, but didn't ask the question of how do you know, as it ran through her mind.

"My mom is a nurse, June! She did teach me a couple things sex Ed didn't."

June just laughed as she covered her face with embarrassment that Terrell had read her mind.

"Take a deep breath," as she exhaled, he inserted himself into her.

"Ouch!" June yelled, but Terrell didn't stop until he was deep inside.

"Do you want me to stop?"

June just shook her head, "No, don't stop." She never removed her hands from her face.

Terrell removed her hands, and placed them behind her back. He kept up the momentum, and they both enjoyed each other for hours. The passion was so overwhelming that tears fell down both their faces afterwards. Completely speechless they both just looked at each other, and Terrell finally asked June if she needed anything. June just shook her head, and rolled over. Terrell got up, to clean himself up, and got a warm towel out the bathroom. When he returns to the bed, she was sitting up. He notices she was wearing the stethoscope neckless he had custom made for her.

"Turn over, and let me clean you up my future doctor."

June smiled, as Terrell cleaned up her now womanly body. Terrell throws the towel across the room, and jumped in the bed with June.

"Terrell I think we should change the sheets, there's blood on them."

"Okay."

After changing the sheets. He cuffed her into his arm, as she slid across the bed.

"I love you girl!" Slipped out of Terrell's mouth, before he knew what he was saying.

"I know," she replied, as she played with her neckless.

"I have to ask!"

"Yes! Terrell."

"What did you really do with the condom?"

"What do you mean, Terrell? I put the condom on."

"No you didn't. I went to clean myself up, and there was no condom."

"Okay, I won't lie, I never actually put it on. I opened it, and begin to! But, I just rolled my fingers down your penis without the condom."

Terrell kissed June on her forehead, and cuffed her tighter. He didn't even ask why, because he was hoping that if he got anyone pregnant, it would be her.

"You do know the dangers of unprotected sex?" June just looked Terrell in his eyes, and rolled on top of him.

"I know! Now, it's my turn to have control." They both rolled under the freshly linen sheets, just to get them dirty again.

20

Aldis jumped up, and buzzed the intercom to Terrell's room early the next morning. "Get up, baby cakes, it's your big day."

When Terrell didn't reply Aldis buzzed again, but this time she just got up, and walked into his empty room. He most has left early. Aldis said, as she woke up Mr. Brown.

"I wonder why he left so early? Maybe rehearsal. Honey go see if his car is outside."

"I don't know." Mr. Brown thought. "Yes, sweetheart, give me a minute."

Rolling out the bed, he went downstairs, checked the newly repaired garage, and behind the house. Walked back into his room, closed the door, and climb back into bed.

"Honey, He's gone."

"Let's just get dressed, and head that way early. That way we'll have better seats, and I can see my baby."

"Okay! But, first shoot him a text, or call, just to be sure he's good."

"Good idea baby." Aldis removed her phone from the charger.

Good Morning! Cupcakes are you already there? 10:00 AM

I'm fine! Mom...   10:15 AM

Son, be safe! We'll see you at the school, in a 1hour 15 min.

Why did you leave so early?   10:15A.M.

......

"He's already at the school." Aldis sighs with relief.

Mr. Brown just smiles! "Trust me! Terrell is just fine. You didn't hear him last night?"

"Yes! I heard him playing on his phone in the middle of the hallway, but after that I was out of it. My work week whore me out. Why? What else happened?"

Mr. Brown shrugged his shoulders. "Nothing babe! Just don't let me forget to tell him to close both vents, and not just one."

"What does that mean? Did he have company?" Mr. Brown just smiles, and asked Aldis to come lay with him for just a minute.

"Honey, I'm about to get dressed."

"Hell! I'm trying to get to Terrells level." Aldis smiled, and climbs back in bed knowing exactly what was about to happen.

"What exactly does that mean, Darnell? Terrell's level, you want to feel young again?"

"Girl, just get over here. I'll show you young again" Soon as Aldis jumped in Darnells arms, her phone rang.

"Hello!"

"Hey Aldis, how are you today?"

"I'm good!" Aldis replied. "What do I owe this call?"

"Well, yet again! June didn't return home last night, and I was wondering if Terrells seen her?"

"No, ma'am. She wasn't here before I went to bed, not to my knowledge. Give me a second I'll ask Darnell, he was up later than me. Hey! Darnell, this is Dawn. June's mother! Did she stop by last night?"

"Yeah, I believe she did."

"Oh, really?" Replied Aldis. "So, June was here last night?"

"Did Terrell ask you, was it ok? How late was it? And I know she didn't stay the night did she?"

"Aldis, relax! It wasn't like that. And, I'm sure they both left for the graduation together."

Aldis just gave Darnell an eye of yeah whatever and continued to talk to Dawn.

"Yes, she was here at some point, from what my husband said, but I'm sure they're both at the graduation now. Terrell isn't here either, he left early for rehearsal."

"Thanks! I'll try texting her again." Dawn hung up the phone with anger.

"Man, this lady really needs to get a handle on her child. Since I've known her, she's always running away, or something. What's really going on in that household? She seems like such a good girl. I wonder why her, and her parents can't get along."

"Yeah, and it's with our son. Aldis!"

"Whatever, Darnell. Let's just get dressed, and go up there to the graduation. I need to speak with this son of mine."

Aldis let these kids be. You act like you ain't never been young, and in love. That's probably why this young lady keeps leaving the house. Let them find their own way.

They're both eighteen for goodness sake, they grown. Cut the
cord.

Darnell got in the shower, and left Aldis lying in the
bed.

21

"These last two months was hell, but I did it. Me and a couple other seniors was the only gradates that still showed up for class after finals. But, I didn't have a choice if I wanted to pass all my classes. Thanks Marie for picking me up, I wasn't taking the bus, and walking was a definite no. Out of all days my battery wants to die."

"Girl you good."

"Damn! This graduation is packed, and thanks Maya for helping me get caught up on my work. You and Frank are really good examples of a friend."

Maya, Marie, Stephanie, and Frank got out the car, and start making their rounds. Frank was only there for support, because he didn't graduate until next year.

"Girl, you good." Replied Maya, "we just wanted to see you walk. Steph you've been through so much, and to graduate will only be a bonus to your worth."

"I know girl, it's been a trip! June bitch ass trying to steal my baby daddy, my parents are m.i.a, and with this job things have been a little rocky."

"Wait! Hold up! You and Terrell got a baby together?"

Oh, shit! Stephanie thought, but didn't voice it. "Yeah! Girl, but don't tell nobody. Some people know just not everybody. Her name is Ally."

"Damn! Girl, how old? When did this happen?" Maya wanted more details.

"She's almost three, which she should be here with Terrells lying family."

"Well, I want to see her when graduation is over."

"Okay," replied Stephanie. "Maya, you see Terrell?"

"No, I haven't. Come to think of it, I haven't seen June either."

"Well, when you do let me know. Me and Frank got something for her ass."

"Frank was in jail for breaking and entering, right?"

"He was, but I bailed him out. Just so we can put this bitch in her place."

"Dang! Steph, you don't like her for real. Do you?"

"Girl no! She makes me sick, but let me see where Frank has wandered off to so we can put our plan in order."

"Okay!" Maya replied "Get at me after graduation."

"Will do."

Stephanie walked away on the hunt for Frank, to be sure their plan was still in motion. Frank was on the other side of the field gossiping in someone else's business.

"Frank, is everything in place?"

"Girl! I can't find June. I seen her parents over there, but she is not here. I got a feeling that her and Terrell ran off.

"Like, Hell! They can't do that. June is valedictorian, and that's not in her behavior.

"Well, no one's seen either one of them. I can't go ask her parents, because Aldis is a couple rolls down from Clay."

"Damn! Frank, why did you break in there anyway?"

"Girl, looking for June. Which, you know John Lace is June's real daddy, not Clay.

"Honey! No, he ain't."

"Oh! Yes, ma'am, but that's not the real tea. When I went over there, to my surprise Aldis was with Lace."

Stephanie mouth just dropped.

"No, sir, she wasn't!"

"When I tell you they were fucking like rabbits. I was like hell no! I waited on the other side of the street. When she finally left I politely got my gun, cause you know a gay man can't go nowhere without his baby. I was about to pull up on Lace, but Terrell pulled up on the other side of the street. I ducked my head so he couldn't see me. Honey, when I tell you his momma went out the back, and he came in the front. When I seen him I got so mad. All I could think about was June, and how she just left me at the 7 11. Then, that if she wasn't around Terrell wouldn't be in the situation he in. So, I drove right over to Clay house. I was gon walk up on Lace, but I figure he didn't have the information I needed.

Anyways! When he opened the door, you can tell he thought I was someone else. But I pushed in. My first intentions were to just talk to June, but when she wasn't home, I wanted answers. I got mad real quick, and wanted to know a couple things. Like if he knew Aldis, if he knew Lace, did he know they were fucking? Yess ma'am I let all the tea out. I mean… They married.

Stephanie just looked at Frank sideways. "Boy, Terrell don't want you. He not even gay. Nowhere close to it."

"Well, we all start off straight."

"The most important thing you should be worried about is Terrell finding out you the one that gave him head that night. Miss Queen, he will beat yo ass, and mine too."

"Anyways, I wasn't concerned with any of that at the time. I was just pissed off about everything that's been happening, and all the drama, and stuff honey."

"Yeah, okay! The graduation is about to start in about forty five minutes. Let's just make sure the circle is in place. So, when we run up on June."

"Okay."

"Where are you going Stephanie?"

"To plant a seed." Stephanie said, with a sinful grin.

Frank watched, as Stephanie walked across the courthouse, and stepped directly to Dawn. Giving her the biggest hug, as she started a conversation. Frank mouth just dropped. Thinking how fearless this bitch was.

"Hi! Mrs. Avery how are you?"

"I'm great sweetheart, how about yourself? I see you in your cap and gown. I'm so proud of you."

"Yes, ma'am. I've been great. I'm just looking for June. I haven't seen her at all today. I tried to text her this morning, but know reply back. I saw where you called me, but I couldn't answer at the rehearsal, which she wasn't there either."

Dawn instantly got nerves. "What do you mean, you haven't seen her. She text me, and told me not to worry, she was here."

"Oh! Well, I haven't seen her yet, but maybe she'll turn up."

Dawn looked over at Aldis, and her and Stephanie walked over with concern.

"Aldis, have you heard from Terrell? This is Stephanie, Junes best friend. She said, she hasn't seen, or heard from June. If she's missing maybe, Terrell knows where she is, so will you please text him once more."

Stephanie extended her hand. "Hi! Aldis. I'm Stephanie, and this must be your husband?"

Stephanie then extended her hand to John Lace, after Aldis wouldn't shake her hand, from being at a lost for words.

Lace responded, "Oh, no sweetheart! That's her husband pointing at Darnell. I just meet Aldis today."

Stephanie just smiled. "I'm so sorry. I just remember seeing her leaving your house, when I rode past the other day. I live about six blocks from you, and I've seen you several times, but didn't know who you were."

Darnell just grabs Stephanie by the arm. "Young lady, I suggest you walk that way before things get real thick around here."

Darnell tried to keep down the confusion, because he knew how Stephanie was, the bigger the crowd the louder the action. And, given that it was a graduation with not only

Terrells peers, but some if not all of his colleagues. He knew Stephanie would have a field day.

"Well, it was nice to meet you guys, I'll go see if I can find June."

Stephanie walked off knowing she had just hit a nerve that would affect both Junes, and Terrell's parents. Darnell pulled Aldis to the side, who was still standing in mute.

"Aldis are you ok?" Replied Darnell. Aldis never took her eyes off Lace.

Dawn looked at Lace with a mouth full of questions. "Lace do you know Aldis? When was she at your house? Is there some truth to what that young lady said?"

Lace didn't say anything, he just looked Aldis in the eyes as she begins to cry.

"Aldis is this true?" Replied Darnell.

Their circle grew tighter, as they was trying to whisper, and understand if there was some kind of love triangle going on.

"Now you know I don't believe shit Stephanie says, so why are crying? It's not true, is it?" Aldis still didn't speak. "What the hell is going on here." Darnell turned, and looked at Lace. "Man, what the fuck! Are you sleeping with my wife?" Before Lace could reply the P.A. Announced, I need everyone to have their seats the graduation is about to begin.

Everyone started to get settled to prepare for the graduation, and find their seats on the open field. In the mist of the confusion Dawns phone rung, and to her surprise it's the principal.

"Hello," Dawn answered fast.

"Yes, Mrs. Avery, this is Mrs. Jones. I am the principal here at Waco high school. We have been on a rampage looking for June. It's been well over two hours, and we haven't seen her. Now, if she's sick, we understand that. But, as the valedictorian, she needed to be here, or at the least your family could've given us a call at your earliest convenience."

"Mrs. Jones we are here at the graduations, and from my understanding June is here. She text me early this morning, and said she was headed to rehearsal. And, that she had left her cap and gown at the school, and would change there. She was getting an early start, and was taking pics with her friends." Dawn jumped out of her seat. "I'll find her!" Dawn hung up the phone, and text Clay.

Hey! Clay, are you with June? 1:00 P.M.

No! I seen her early this morning, with some guy headed in the direction of the school, but I thought you knew. 1:05 P.M.

Dawn went straight over to Aldis. "Listen, I don't give a shit what you, and Lace did at this moment. I just need to know where is my child is. Please call Terrell she's with him."

Aldis pulls out her phone, and calls Terrell. She looks down to a field full of black gowns, and black caps. For the first time Aldis was baffled, about the situation. She slowly turned her head to scan the crowd, when she notices Stephanie was waving her hand in her directions, and laughing with Frank. Before she could react Terrell answered.

"Hello!"

"Terrell, where the hell are you? Do you have June with you? And is that Ally I hear in the background? What is going on I thought you was here at the graduation?"

"Yep! I was at the graduation mother, but after talking things over with June last night, or should I say early this morning we decided to leave the graduation up to the parents this year. Y'all the ones that need to grow up."

"Terrell, please! Where are y'all going? I'm beyond worried, and so are the Averys. Terrell, you have someone else's child. Please think about her family. Aldis didn't receive a response. "Hello!" The operator informed Aldis that if she'd like to make a call to please hang up, and call again.

Aldis storms down several lines, and snatch Stephanie out of her seat. The Avery's followed behind, as Darnell did the same.

"You little bitch! You knew exactly what you were doing, and I'm sick of your bullshit. Now, you tell me where my child is before I beat your ass right here, right now!" Mrs. Brown yelled. "I know you're the main cause of all of this drama, and I want answers. So, tell me where are they, and I mean now!"

Aldis threw Stephanie on the ground, and bowed up her fist. Darnell, and Clay tried to hold her back as the crowd was in an uproar, and couldn't focus on the announcer. Security ran in Aldis direction, and so did the cops.

Stephanie just laughed as she said, "life's a bitch ain't it. Now you feel how I've felt. Now get yo hands off me." Stephanie snatched her hands away, and the Avery's, and John Lace stepped back.

"That's it," replied Aldis as she begins to swing on Stephanie.

"Aldis, if you hit my fucking daughter, you will have hell to pay."

Aldis turned around shocked, as Clay, Lace, Darnell, Dawn, and this unfamiliar lady surrounded her, by the police.

"Mom?" Stephaine replied, with a blank stare. "You're here?"

Acknowledgment!

I have to give a great acknowledgment to my Savior. The Lord Jesus Christ, without him I am nothing. He gave me this gift of writing, and I will never take it for granted. He placed me in an atmosphere where I could be myself, and focus on my craft. I, also have to give a big thank you to all my family, my support system. My mom (Jeanie), father (Brian), and my sibling (Otha, and Jennifer). My wonder husband (George), and my awesome children (Pierre, Jacob, and Jayla). The love from my entire family is completely amazing, and has always been. Also giving thanks to everyone who supported me throughout this journey (Tracy Lyons,

Ann Gardner, and Krista Wells) Just to name a few.

It's been a long road, but it was a great ride one!

Sneak Peek... Come on, Let's Look.

Stephanie's Revenge

Rage, Disappointment, & Rebirth

Stephanie finally makes it back to her apartment, after a very stressful graduation. "I am completely blown away that my parents showed up! Why? I don't know. Should I care? Right now, at this moment, I really don't. I mean, damn! I know it's been close to three years since I've seen my dad, and maybe a year for mom. How dare they just show up like that, no warning, no nothing.

Then Terrell runs off with that little bitch June. I hope they get in another car accident, together this time, and die. Wait! My baby with them, so never mind. Damn! Now, that's a tough pill to swallow. I have a daughter, and I will never see her again."

Stephanie looked over her balcony, where she always goes for solitude, and took a deep breath. She finally got enough nerve and stood on the edge. I feel like flying, she thought as she spread open her arms like an eagle. I mean, what do I have to live for?

Stephaine jumped down, and came to her senses. I love my life, I can't do this. But, the little voice in her mind told her to go for it.

"Okay," she answered.

She places one foot on the edge, and pulled herself up. She stood still, her arms were still spread wide, and her head facing the heavens.

Lord, if you are real, and if you hear me. I'm asking you to please have someone save me, before I take this leap. I feel my Lord, like I have no hope left. Like my life has completely gone into shambles, and there is no reason for me to live. At this point you are the only hope I have, and if no one comes to save me, please save my soul.

Stephanie stood in silence for a minute like an idled statue. The countdown began from ten. The wind begins to pick up, and the breeze made her feet stagnant. "Oh, Shit!" She yelled. I might as well let go...

To be continued.....

Well, well, well! If you enjoyed please follow my postings on "Exclusive Protection" Facebook page. You can leave a comment, share, or even leave a funny emoji(lol) whatever you choose. Also, for more book updates on what's next to come join my email group: @ julietmcjackson.com

Thanks in advance!

Juliet Jackson!

www.ingramcontent.com/pod-product-compliance
Lightning Source LLC
Chambersburg PA
CBHW030925260626
47169CB00002B/378